Twists
Of
Fate

MARY JANE FORBES

Todd Book Publications

TWISTS OF FATE

ISBN: 978-0692202197 (sc)
Printed in the United States of America
Todd Book Publications: 4/2014
Second Edition: 9/2017
Port Orange, Florida

Author photo: Ami Ringeisen Floyd
Cover design 2018 by Angie: pro_ebookcovers

Locations

Maine / Massachusetts

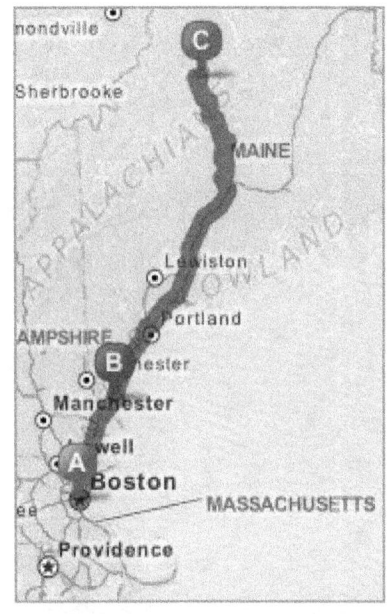

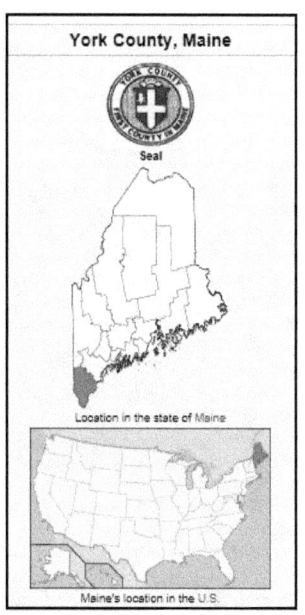

A: Boston
B: York
C: Moosehead Lake

CAST

From The Witness
Dr. Maria Grayson
   Morgan Grant (alias)
Marianne Grayson:
  Maria's Mom

Feds
Agent Alex Donovan

Florida Friends
Elizabeth Stitchway, PI
Manny Salinas, PI

North Carolina
Steven & Sylvia Caldwell
Trixie Flintrock
Janie Flintrock

York Maine
Dr. Joe (Barly)
  Bartholomew
Chenoa Bartholomew
Stella Trent
Doc Waldo Whistle
Chief Keith Roth
Detective Rodney Hall

San Francisco Caper
Susan & Jeffrey Sinclair
Detective Patrick
       Steele

Boston
Cookie
Kim Trotter

Twists

Of

Fate

Chapter 1

Cortez, Florida
Goodbye

THE PATTY SUE FISHING charter sliced through the gentle waves stirring up the salty air of the Gulf waters off the western shore of Florida. Dr. Maria Grayson stood at the stern staring at the Cortez dock receding from view.

Mac was dead!

An experienced commercial fisherman, he drowned in a freak accident. How could this have happened to Mac Macintyre, her husband of two years?

Dressed all in white, a shiver ran up Maria's arms under her cardigan sweater, elbows jerking into her rib cage. The soft wool of her slacks rippled with the breeze. Jenny, her Golden Retriever, leaned into her leg. Maria's fingers stretched d
own stroking the dog's silky head—companions comforting one another.

Mac was dead!

Danny Macintyre, Mac's father, slumped next to Maria, his hands grasping the iron rail to steady his late-sixties bag of bones. Feeling Maria's arm shift, he laid his leathery, arthritic fingers over the soft knuckles of her hand holding the rail. Her hand turned up under his touch, holding tight to Danny as she continued to stare out over the wake.

Her two closest friends, private investigators Elizabeth Stitchway and Manny Salinas, stood on her other side. Manny's arm around Elizabeth's shoulders, her head gently tilted to his protective frame. The pair had tied the knot the year before Maria and Mac were married. The two mourners, flanking Maria and her dog, were dressed in black, their hands grasping the rail as the Patty Sue cut through the waves to the spot believed to be Mac's final resting place.

Mac's loyal crew and faithful friends—Sissy, an Asian with a scar down his cheek, and Shrimp, a large black man with a piece of flesh cut from his calf—were piloting the sport fishing charter. They chose to dress in uniform: tan trousers and shirts topped with black leather jackets. Macintyre & Son Fishing Charters was embroidered in white on the black leather as well as on the pockets of their tan shirts. The fishermen chatted quietly, Sissy's hands gripping the wheel steering the boat to the location, as best as he could determine, where three weeks prior their skipper lost his life trying to save two sport fishermen.

———

THE FISHERMEN HAD CHARTERED the Patty Sue for a day of excitement out at sea. That day started as today, bright and sunny. A storm had suddenly gathered, chasing the Patty Sue back to the village of Cortez. But the storm overtook the boat. The waves thwarted every move Mac made to outrun the powerful wind and angry waters. The two sport fishermen had foolishly doffed their lifejackets in the excitement of reeling in a mighty grouper and a red snapper. The men lost their footing on the slippery deck and were washed overboard by a sudden surge of a great wave. Mac had immediately cut the engines, yelled instructions to Sissy, his lone crewman that day, to tie down the ropes on the life preservers then to toss them out as he dove in the water.

One fisherman desperately lunged at the round tube, missed, lunged again grabbing hold, gagging on water filling his throat. Sissy pulled him to the boat, both struggling, fighting the waves, then the fisherman managed to roll one leg up over the side. Sissy's large hands held fast to the man's arm scraping his body over the edge, his torso falling onto the deck, gasping for air.

Sissy then turned to help Mac and the other fisherman whose arms were flailing, trying to grasp the second life preserver. Mac hollered at the man to stop thrashing at the water. The man, slipping under the waves, surfacing, fighting for air, didn't hear Mac. Gathering all his strength, Mac shoved the man to the tube. His arm punched through the center, circled the tube in a death grip.

Mac screamed, screamed again ... disappeared under the crash of a fifteen-foot wave.

Sissy tightened his lifejacket, dove into the swelling waves where he had last seen Mac. A great white shark swam by Sissy, his jaw clamped shut on his prize, as Sissy's eyes filled with bloody water.

Horrified, Sissy surfaced hollering for a life preserver, gagging, his lungs screaming for air. Fighting the waves he made a grab for the tube the fisherman threw out to him, clutching the tube to his chest. The two fishermen on deck pulled Sissy alongside the boat, grabbed his arms slithering him over the edge to safety.

Choking, vomiting water over the side, tears streamed from the Asian's eyes over his sun-beaten leathery face. He knew the search was futile as he climbed to the flying bridge, yelling at the fishermen to watch for Mac. Engaging the motors Sissy circled the Patty Sue in wide swaths, his eyes peeled for any glimpse of Mac. He saw nothing only crashing waves washing over the deck.

The storm intensified.

Sobbing, hunched over the wheel, fearing the vessel would be swamped, Sissy turned the Patty Sue to the east, to Cortez. Tormented, he abandoned the search. An hour later the Patty Sue smacked against the dock's battered pilings.

Danny, leaning into the wind, rain pelting his rubber poncho, arms clinging to a post on the dock, waiting for the Patty Sue, was ready to help the fishermen from the boat. A veteran of the vagaries of the weather on the Gulf, his bones told him his son would have a fight to bring the Patty Sue back in one piece and he was ready to lend assistance.

With the fishing party safely off the boat, the Patty Sue safely lashed to the rings along the dock, Danny joined Sissy on the flying bridge. The men huddled against the pelting rain, the wind whipping their yellow slickers. Danny, lips drawn down, eyebrows scrunched, stared at Sissy's tear-stained face trying to comprehend what the man was telling him.

Climbing down from the bridge the two men stepped to the stern, heads down, fists clutching the rail. The storm swarmed around their bodies bent into the wind and rain as they unsuccessfully choked back their pain.

———

"THIS IS IT!" SISSY YELLED from the flying bridge. He cut the twin engines to idle setting the Patty Sue to drift slowly with the tide.

Maria looked out over the dazzling water, then up to the heavenly blue sky. A few puffs of white cotton languished overhead. So, this is the place Mac took his last breath. How had the past two years come to this moment? She stood, the handle of the wicker basket of red rose petals over her arm swung to the rhythm of the ripples caressing the Patty Sue's hull.

Shifting the basket next to Danny, he softly offered a simple prayer. "May you rest in peace, son." The words catching in his throat as he whispered, "Amen." His gnarled fingers plucked several petals from the basket, dropping them over the side into the water.

Maria did the same—caressing the soft velvety petals, raising them to her cheek, breathing in their sweet, delicate scent. She pressed one to her lips … if only things could have been different. Extending her hand she released the petals' fleeting beauty to the gentle breeze, folding into a cocoon around the memory of the fisherman who so loved the sea.

Shifting the basket to Liz and Manny, they both freed several petals to the gentle waves ruffling against the Patty Sue.

Sissy and Shrimp had scampered down from the bridge. Their rough calloused fingers scooped the remains of the roses from the basket, awkwardly tossing them into the water.

Danny looked at Maria, raised his brows—did she want to say something?

Maria shook her head. Everything had been said the day Mac left in anger. His last day. Now she was saying goodbye to her husband, throwing flowers on his watery grave. How did it feel to die? Did he struggle to fight off the shark? Of course he did. Did he call out for her or was his voice strangled with unsaid words? Did he feel pain? She prayed to God that he didn't, that peace came quickly. *I should have done more, tried harder to rescue our marriage.* Setting the empty basket on the deck, she wrapped her empty arms around her body. Looking up, she nodded to Sissy and Shrimp who had returned to the bridge. The Patty Sue's engines came to life. She swung around, headed back to Cortez.

And, that was that!

———

DANNY SAT WITH MARIA on a bench in the stern, the bench where fishermen watch their lines for signs of a bite. Jenny lay to her side, her muzzle resting on her white sandals. The sun warmed Maria's skin as she stared at the Patty Sue's wake. Maria threaded her arm around Danny's. "I'm leaving, Danny."

"Not surprised ... but, sad at the thought. Where would you be heading?"

"North. Strange isn't it? Three years ago I was a witness, whisked away under the Federal Witness Protection Program—a star witness to a drug cartel murder. I suddenly began life as a different person, unknown even to me ... Dr. Morgan Grant. Morgan fit in with the York locals. They're rugged in Maine, yet at the same time warm, at least to me. Of course, doctors gain the trust of patients unless you give them a reason not to. They instinctively believe a doctor will help them."

"Maine ... long way away. I'll miss you, Maria. When are you leaving?"

"When we bump against the dock ... it will be my last time on the Patty Sue ... on the waterfront in Cortez. Which brings me to a couple of questions I have for you. You and I are now partners in the Macintyre and Son Charter business—your half and mine from Mac. Do you want to take over the business?"

"I think not. Not pushing seventy. Commercial fishing is dangerous, and the charter business is demanding. Requires the care of a younger man."

"How about we give the Patty Sue to Sissy and Shrimp? I believe Mac would want them to have her. They could be partners. You would remain a business partner, a consultant."

"Funny you should say that. I came up with the same idea only yesterday. I was going to ask you … great minds … or something." Danny chuckled, his arm tightening briefly on Maria's. "Except for the consulting thing. I have enough to see me through … through until I join Mac. Let the boys run the business. With the Patty Sue free and clear, they'll be able to buy a second boat. Bring in enough money to make a go of it. I know Sissy has his eyes on one. Those boys have the same passion for the sea as Mac had." A sudden wash of emotion gripped Danny. Sucking in several gulps of air, he steadied himself.

"How about the house, Danny? I've packed everything I'm taking with me. Same house you and your wife lived in."

"It's special to me. I'll say that for it. Just a few blocks from the docks, my buddies. I'd like that, Maria."

"Good, because I already deeded it to you. The papers are on the kitchen table waiting for your signature." This time it was Maria who was suddenly awash with sadness.

She was alone—no family, no brothers, no sisters. Her mother suffered from advanced Alzheimer's and her father … well, he had disappeared before she was born. If she fell into the water, sinking to the bottom of the sea, no one would care. She would not be missed. Happily ever after only occurs in fairy tales.

Her violet eyes rose to the sky, a gust of wind lifting a lock of her auburn hair as she whispered a plea to the heavens that what she was feeling wasn't true, that her life had no value. Or did it? She felt a sudden spasm, trying to shed the dark thoughts, trying to grab on, hold tight, to a fuzzy, fleeting image of a new life ahead. She was a doctor, she helped people, she saved people. If she didn't have a family … then by God she'd create one … adoption, sperm donor. There were ways.

She felt Liz take her hand as she sat down on the bench. Manny, too. "What are your plans, Maria?" Liz asked.

"I'm leaving. Going north. I'll let you know. I'm at a turning point. I can't stay here. I have no one. But strange as it seems, Maine is calling me. The weather is not idyllic—beautiful summers, harsh winters that test the spirit. I have contacts there. As I see it, I can pick up this life or pick up that life."

"Listen to me, girlfriend, Manny and I won't hear of you disappearing from us again. If we don't hear from you in a few weeks, we'll be racing north to find you. Don't forget, we're private eyes, we can find anyone, right Manny?"

"Dang right. And don't wait too long. You know Elizabeth Stitchway, AKA Stitch, when she sets her mind to something, well, let's just say she has a nose like a bloodhound. I swear she does." Manny chuckled, leaning in with a puff of air on his wife's ear.

"You two are treasures. Don't worry, I won't forget. You'll be the first ones I call when I settle in."

The Patty Sue bumped against the dock's weathered pilings, a signal to everyone onboard that it was time to get on with their lives. Safely tied to the dock, the ripples in the harbor causing a gentle sway of the vessel, Maria hustled to the steps Sissy had positioned for his passengers to disembark. She called over her shoulder asking everyone to wait a minute. She wanted to capture them on her camera. Capture their images, capture this day, capture the boat Mac had cared for all his life.

Fishing her new little red camera out of her tote, she first fastened the lens on Danny, catching the sadness in his eyes. He had wanted a grandson. He'd endured tragedies before—the loss of his first love, Patty Sue, the boat's namesake, the loss of his wife, Regina and now the loss of his son.

Seeing Danny through the lens, her breath caught in her chest. I will not let that happen to me. I will have a baby somehow. We will be a family.

Moving the lens slightly to the left, to her friends Liz and Manny, she caught them smiling, a thin smile, topped with sad eyes. Liz looked up at Manny, basking in the light of his eyes full of love for her. The lens caught every movement.

Pointing the camera up at the flying bridge, she snapped the Asian and the black man several times. Sadness? No … wait … a playful gesture as they punched each other's arm. Danny had told them of the gift. They were the new skippers of the Patty Sue, wonderment still showing on their faces like little boys at Christmas opening a present they never thought possible. Danny's words were still ringing in their ears. Had they heard him right? Yes, they did. Maria would send the papers to Danny, and he would give the new partners the documents, proof of ownership. The Patty Sue was theirs.

The eye of the camera caught it all. Everything stored in memory.

Lowering the camera, dropping it back into the tote, Maria waved. Threw a kiss to each standing together in the stern, just above the lettering: *Patty Sue*. Maria turned, touched her thigh for Jenny to follow. A soft bark urged her mistress on as she slowly walked away on the rough hewn boards of the dock.

Leaving her life with Mac, Maria picked up her stride, Jenny trotting ahead, both eager to get going.

Chapter 2

STAND AFTER STAND OF palm trees and palmetto bushes, acres of grassy fields where prized horses frolicked freely, passed in and out of view as Maria's white and black Mini Cooper ticked off the miles, still way more miles ahead than what was left behind.

Leaving Cortez, driving north on I-75, she had an overwhelming desire to see her mother at Sunrise House. Maybe stay a couple of days—it had been six months since her last visit. A visit that did not go well. Marianne Grayson had acknowledged her daughter briefly and then slipped back into the shadows of Alzheimer's.

With one hand on the wheel, her cell in the other, she called the director of the home letting her know she would be visiting her mother tomorrow. Mrs. Trebly said it was iffy whether Marianne would know her. Some days were better than others. She could only pray for a good day.

With the temperature rising—a hot, humid, May afternoon— Maria pulled into the first rest stop changing into tan shorts topped with a white T-shirt. She pulled her hair into a tight ponytail, poking it through the hole in the back of a black ball cap. Feeling cooler, she slipped on her white sneakers. After taking Jenny for a quick run, she climbed back into the car and continued up the highway.

Maria glanced over at Jenny her black nose twitching through the open crack of the window. "We'll stop tonight in Tallahassee. With a fresh start in the morning we'll be in New Orleans by early afternoon," she said patting Jenny's golden fur. Sighing, she picked up her red camera from the console. Lowering her window, she snapped a few shots of the palm trees.

Maria flashed a big grin at her dog. Jenny reciprocated with a toothy grin. It was a trick the dog's original owner had taught her. With the *teeth* command Jenny would curl her lip into a snarl, or a grin, depending on how the observer took it. Maria taught her to *grin* in response to a big toothy smile, sometimes causing strangers to marvel if they flashed a wide grin at the dog telling her how pretty she was.

Up at dawn the next day, a hearty breakfast at the McDonald's drive thru consisting of a large coffee and an Egg McMuffin for herself and two burger patties for Jenny, Maria was back on Interstate 10. She began snapping pictures showing her progress— *Welcome to Alabama; Welcome to Mississippi, Welcome to Louisiana,* and finally after five hours, *New Orleans City Limit.*

———

IT WAS A PRETTY ROOM that Marianne Grayson called home. The walls were a sunny yellow, a nice backdrop for the white French Provincial bureau. A quilt with nosegays of spring flowers appliquéd in yellow, blue, and pink, covered the bed. The quilt Maria bought when her mother first took up residence at the home.

A woman sat next to the window across the room from Maria. The woman continued to stare at Maria, eyes devoid of any recognition that her daughter sat three feet away.

Maria leaned back in a flowery slip covered chair, crossed her legs. Forcing her lips into a congenial smile, she chatted softly about the good times mother and daughter had shared, beginning her sentences with ... *remember when* ... hoping to trigger a response.

An attendant, her curly gray hair framing her face, shuffled in, balancing a tray with a small carafe, two china cups, and a couple of lemon cookies. "Miss Marianne enjoys an afternoon cup of tea especially with a visitor, don't you dear?" The attendant, knowing there would be no response, bustled out the door to distribute another tray of treats to the residents on her list.

Maria poured the tea, setting her mother's cup on the table next to her chair, continued her banter of happier times.

Jenny laid on the floor next to Maria, her eyes glancing up whenever her name was mentioned along with a lazy thump of her tail on the beige carpet.

Finished with her tea, Maria set the empty cup beside her mother's untouched cup. Kissing her mother on the cheek, she left, Jenny trotting by her side. On the way out, she told Mrs. Trebly that she'd return in the morning hoping a new day would bring some clarity to her mother's mind.

Unfortunately, that was not the case. After sharing a cup of breakfast tea with the woman in the sunny yellow room with the flowered quilt, Maria stood to leave reaching out to touch her mother's cheek. The woman scrunched her face slapping the stranger's hand away.

Maria, a wounded look in her eyes, paused, then kissed the air above her mother's forehead. "Bye, Mom. I love you."

Chapter 3

———

STOMPING ON THE GAS PEDAL, Maria turned onto the highway trying to expunge the blank stare from the woman in the sunny yellow room. Racing down the highway out of Louisiana, she finally let up on the gas, setting the cruise control to the speed limit.

Leaving the woman in the sunny room wasn't hard. Leaving the woman she remembered as her mother was heartbreaking. The miles passed under the tires of her car, the hum of the engine serving as a tonic to the ache in the pit of her stomach—images of Mac and her mother fading in the distance.

Turning the radio up, Maria and Jenny belted out country songs as they drove through Tennessee. Tears ran down her face as she sang along with Loretta Lynn's rendition of the *Coal Miner's Daughter*.

Looking in the rearview mirror, she scolded herself for letting her emotions run wild. "Caffeine, that's what the doctor orders. Hey what, Jenny? You want to stretch your legs, too?"

Exchanging glances with Jenny, Maria turned into the rest area, parking under a stand of maple trees. Snapping the leash on Jenny's collar the pair trotted around the grass-lined parking lot stopping here and there for Jenny to do her business or to follow a powerful scent.

"Time to make some plans, girl. Wait while I get my coffee and a bottle of water for you. Then, we're calling Stella." Maria tied Jenny to a tree then sprinted to the snack counter.

Sitting back at a picnic table, Jenny enjoying a doggie cookie with an occasional slurp of water, Maria pulled her cell from her tote.

"Hi, Stel. Surprise! Jenny and I are taking a break at a rest stop … we're on our way to Maine."

"What? How far are you? My God, it's been two years, Morgan—"

"Maria, Stella. My name is Maria."

"Oh, yeah. Sorry, I forgot. It's just such a shock to hear from you out of the blue like this. Is Mac with you?"

Maria sucked in her breath dropping the phone, a tremor growing in her fingers. She hadn't told anyone outside of Cortez about Mac. Her eyes darted from the trees, to a father with an infant in a backpack, to cars racing up the highway. Of course, people were going to ask about Mac.

She picked up her cell from the weathered table. "Stel, you there?"

"Yeah, what happened?"

"I dropped the phone."

"So, is Mac with you?"

"… Mac's dead," Maria whispered.

"What? Did I hear you right?"

"Yes. An accident … out in the Gulf … two months ago."

"An accident? How? Never mind. We'll talk when you get here. Drive carefully … are you sure you're okay to drive?"

"Stel, can we stay with you for a couple of days until I find a house to rent?"

"Oh my God, of course. Who's we?"

"Jenny and I."

"Does anyone know you're coming? Dr. Farnsworth? Anyone?"

"No, and I want to keep it that way. I should be in York in three days. If you see a little house for rent, two bedrooms, or maybe three, cut it out of the newspaper, or make a note with the address and the contact number."

"Sure. Drive safe … Maria, it'll be great to see you."

"Back at 'cha… soon, Stel."

Maria closed her cell, dropping it in her tote with the red camera. "Jenny, Stella wanted to know if I was okay to drive. That's a laugh. I'm not okay to do much of anything. Come on let's get going. I have one more call to make but I'll make it once we're on the road."

Settled back in the car, Maria turned out of the parking lot and back onto the highway. Again the Mini Cooper chewed up the miles, but Maria wasn't in a hurry to transition from one life to start another. She needed time, but it was nice to hear Stella's voice. Such a good friend.

"Look at that, Jenny. Welcome to Pennsylvania."

Jenny flopped her tail once and then turned her nose to the lush green countryside whizzing by the window.

Taking a deep breath, Maria retrieved her cell. Glancing from the road to the directory, she tapped Donovan's name.

"Agent Donovan."

"Hi, Alex. It's Maria."

"Maria?"

"Dr. Maria Grayson, otherwise known as Dr. Morgan Grant," she said with a giggle. *Wow, that felt good.* She almost laughed.

"Maria. Good heavens. How are you?"

"Not great but I'm working on it."

"How's that fisherman of yours?"

There it was again. Those outside of Cortez won't know about Mac. Get used to it, Maria. Take a breath and answer him.

"He's dead. Lost at Sea. An accident. I'm calling from my car … on my way to Maine. The place you took me for protection. I guess I should thank you."

"Maria, I'm sorry … about Macintyre."

Nothing to say. Ignore his sympathy. "Alex, I'm calling to ask for your help. Can you purge Morgan Grant? Replace her with Maria Grayson, the real me—all the fake records you created for Morgan Grant with my real history—not Washington State, but New Orleans, Tulane, my doctor's degree? Nothing needs to be done regarding my position at Manatee Memorial Hospital in Florida. Everything there is correct—Dr. Grayson. Also, please check that the Maine licensing Board has me listed as Dr. Maria Grayson."

"I'll take care of it, Maria. May take me a few days, a week or two. It will take a little longer to put you back together than it did when … when we created your new identity."

"Thanks, Alex. I'll check back with you when I'm settled. In the meantime you have my cell number."

"Maria, I'm sorry …"

"It's a long story, Alex. I'm about three days out of York. I'll call you. Bye."

Dr. Maria Grayson swiped at a tear. "Where did that come from? Why now?"

The tremor in her hand kicked up again. She had kept a tight rope around her nerves, but the rope was easing, releasing her feelings of loss, of failure. Oh yes, she still had to deal with the overwhelming feeling of having failed Mac.

She looked at the thirty-nine-year-old woman in the rearview mirror. *What do you do if your life has no meaning?*

Chapter 4

York, Maine

A FLASH OF GOLD FUR darted from the car at the same time that Stella flew out the door running up to Maria, wrapping her arms around her friend in a fierce hug, happy tears rolling down their cheeks. Stella, pushing away to arms length, checked Maria head to toe. "You look fabulous, Maria. There, I remembered your name ... done with the Morgan thing. A little dark under the eyes—nothing I can't fix." Her laugh was infectious. Beaming, she entwined her arm through Maria's, steering her to the front door. Stella's long, wavy, dark-brown hair swishing side to side in response to her movements, all five feet of her.

They both laughed at Jenny barking, dashing from tree to tree. Ah, freedom.

Maria filled her lungs, breathing in the cool May air. "It's wonderful to be here, to see you. You look terrific by the way," she said, pulling Stella into a tight hug. "I couldn't believe your text message: *found you a house*. Did you get the key?"

"You bet. I have it right here." Stella dangled a gold key attached to the realtor's card. "Want something to drink or go straight to the house?"

"Do you mind ... I'm anxious to see the place? The pictures were ... too good to be true, except for one thing."

"What's that?"

"It's so big. Don't get me wrong, I'm ready for big ... but maybe not for a few months."

"I get you, but it's not forever. You're house-sitting while the owners spend two years traveling. So how bad can it be … wild parties …

"Oh, I doubt that. Come on. Here comes Jenny, tongue hanging out from running. It was tough being cooped up in the car. She's going to be crazy about the woodsy surroundings I saw on the website."

Standing on the top step of her parent's house, Stella grinned, a big ear-to-ear grin. Another hug and then the friends whirled around to the car, missing Jenny's smile.

———

THE HOUSE WAS WAY, way better than the photos—a cozy green-clapboard cape built in 1978. A large bush by the front door infused the air with the scent of lilac.

Inside the pine floorboards glowed, polished to a warm patina, surrounded by white plastered walls. The kitchen's honey-pine cupboards faced a breakfast nook tucked in a bay window. Opposite the bay window was an archway leading to the dining room with a cherry harvest table and eight ladder-back chairs tucked up to it. The living room ceiling vaulted to the heavens.

Turning around, Maria looked up to see a filigreed wrought iron railing outlining the loft with two bedrooms and a bath between. A third bedroom was on the main floor along with a smaller room the owners had set up as an office.

The furniture was comfortable New England—overstuffed couches protected with flowery slipcovers, wing-back chairs flanking the stone fireplace. Oriental rugs added warmth in the living room and dining room. Upstairs the bedrooms were cozy spaces grounded with braided rugs, circled with dressers, beds, side tables in pine, cherry, and light oak. A bowl in each bedroom provided a distinct scent of roses in one and lavender in the other. Charming, all!

"What do you think?" Stella plopped down on a quilt covering an antique spool bed.

"I think it's fantastic … but as I said … much too big for one person."

Hearing Jenny bark at the front door, Maria hustled down the stairs to let her in. Exhausted, panting, her eyes were bright from chasing her favorite animal—she was back in squirrel-filled woods. Maria smiled down at the dog smiling back at her. The house too big for one person but perfect for a frisky retriever. "A beautiful dog. Yes you are," Maria said giving Jenny a good back rub.

"Well, the rental agent had a couple other places. I looked at them but they just weren't you. But we can call her." Stella retrieved her cell phone from her purse.

"Wait. Don't call her, Stel. I want to ask you something."

"Shoot."

"Do you like children, little children, well … babies?"

"Ah … yes … one, maybe two. But a kindergarten full I'm out. Why? Oh my God, don't tell me you're going to start a daycare—"

Maria chuckled. "Never. While I'm finishing my residency—"

"Residency? You're already a doctor. A surgeon. What's with the residency?"

"So much has happened, Stel. I'm trying to figure out who I am, what I want. The past few years changed me."

"Listen, Maria, you have every right to be confused."

"After I married Mac, I decided on a specialty. I've been working on my residency—pediatrics. One more year to go to qualify for the Maine Boards and my license as a pediatrician." Maria dug her nails into her palms, paced over the living room's soft Oriental rug stopping in front of Stella, stopping her stream of babble that had built up over the miles since she left Florida.

"Luckily everything I've done before I started training for pediatrics counted. One day, on a whim, I called the director at York Hospital to see if they had an opening. She was surprised to hear from me. She didn't have an opening but referred me to White Pines Memorial Hospital, west of I-95. They were having difficulty trying to find a Pediatric doctor to replace one who left without notice. So I called the Director at White Pines. We had a long chat … really a telephone interview. Hearing my background, she offered me a three-month trial position, provided my records were in order, and of course she would check my references at York. If all goes well, the position is mine and I can finish my residency there."

"Thank God there was an opening … they'll be lucky to have you."

"And … I want a baby. Mac and I tried … for a while. But our schedules, mine really, interfered with our lives."

"Whoa, that's a lot of information … what are you saying? I thought you and Mac were head over heels in love."

"It's a long story, and not for today. So—"

"So you think a baby will make you whole?" Stella had curled up on the couch, watching Maria morph from one person to another—a doctor, wanna-be mother, widow.

Maria's fingers traced over the gleaming cherry library table next to the staircase. The vision of a baby, a family, was fuzzy. She hadn't managed to bring it into her mind clearly. Maybe it wasn't meant to be. She shook her head. "Maybe in time. I tell you, Stel, working with the babies over the last two years was wonderful. Maybe that was one part of the problem between Mac and I … I hated to go home, hated to be torn away from the nursery at the hospital. The babies were so tiny, so helpless."

"But babies grow up, Maria."

"Yeah. God knows I'm sure it won't be smooth. Teenage years scare me, but it's only a few years. This house will be perfect to start with. Then, when the time is right, buy my own place."

"Given up on falling in love again? There are lots of men who would die to be close to the beautiful, auburn-haired doctor with sultry violet eyes."

Maria's head snapped up, her eyes wide, connecting with Stella's warm brown pupils. "Stel, move in with me. You said you're not thrilled about living with your parents. And you haven't exactly made a move on the male-female relationship arena either unless you've been keeping something from me. But I haven't given you a chance—I've been going on—"

"Oh my. I don't know." Stella popped off the couch, her eyes glancing around the room, up at the loft. "Wonder if you meet someone … I guess I could move out."

"Or vice versa. If you meet someone, then, of course, you'd set up housekeeping with him in your own place. In the meantime, we'll be our own little support group, like sisters. Let's give it a try, Stel. A few months, a year. Then we reassess. What do you say?"

Chapter 5

———

WOULD SHE SEE him today?

A smile formed on her lips immediately followed by a clutch in her chest. How could she even think of Barly after failing Mac? Admittedly, every day she had glanced around when she was in the hospital—when stopping for a snack in the hospital cafeteria, when the elevator door slid open wondering if he would be standing there. She knew his practice was now affiliated with White Pines, but did he know she was back? He must know. Her name was posted as a new resident on the pediatric floor. The only conclusion—he didn't want to see her. She had hurt him once, so why set himself up for pain again.

Maria's eyes sought the sun streaming in the window. She had much to be thankful for. Stella was a Godsend. They moved into the house the same day Maria signed the rental agreement. Stella insisted on sharing the expenses but Maria insisted the rental was to be in her name. That way, either one of them was free to change the arrangement.

Stella was so happy to be out of her parent's house she would have agreed to almost anything. She was a bright spirit, shooing away any lingering feelings Maria had of being alone. Born of a French mother and African American father, she was a beautiful woman with deep olive skin. A year younger than Maria, divorced at twenty-four, and a disastrous relationship with a drug dealer, she was ecstatic to have some privacy.

Life settled quickly into a routine—taking Jenny out for a run, returning to shower, passing Stella in the hall. The two would high-five, wish each other a good day and then part with coffee cups in hand. Stella, the manager of an office supply outlet, took Jenny to the store with her. The dog would snuggle on her blanket behind the counter, her eyes darting around, checking each new customer.

Maria drove to the hospital to care for the tiny people in her charge in the maternity nursery and then spend several hours on the pediatric floor. Her routine constantly changed with emergencies, schedule disruptions, and, as the new kid, pulling the night shift.

But all told, the two women had fallen into an easy, warm, comfortable pattern, enjoying each other's company and swapping stories of their day over a glass of wine. Even as the temperature rose with the approach of summer, they would light the gas logs in the fireplace for the warm ambiance, Jenny luxuriating, in front of the hearth.

Still, Maria hadn't seen Barly. Naturally he would be busy with his private practice, only scheduled at the hospital for cardiac surgeries.

Dr. Richard Farnsworth, the doctor who took Morgan Grant on as a nurse practitioner when she arrived in York three years ago, was unaware at the time that she was under Federal protection, and unaware that she was not a nurse but an accredited surgeon. Farnsworth made it a point to stop by the White Pines' maternity nursery. He had greeted her with a warm fatherly hug. Harriett, his office manager, had given him strict instructions, that morning when he left for the hospital, to tell Maria that Harriett expected her to stop by soon and to bring Jenny. After all, Harriett had dog-sat Jenny on numerous occasions. This was her last week before retiring so he'd better not forget or else she'd have to track her down herself.

The week after Farnsworth's visit, donning a fresh set of blue scrubs, Maria hustled to the nursery. Twins had been delivered during the night, preemies—a four-pound boy and a little over three-pound girl. Maria's heart lurched seeing the baby girl, so tiny in her incubator.

Her hands cleansed with disinfectant, Maria stepped to the baby's life-support-system, gently inserted her hand, softly touching the preemie's tiny fingers. The baby's hand jerked in the air at the intrusion, then the tiny fingers relaxed on Maria's finger. The baby's eyes opened, her little feet giving a kick.

"Maria?"

Maria's finger didn't move from under the baby's grasp, only her eyes rose, her breathing stopped, nerves pinging throughout her system, his familiar cologne faintly circling her head. From the sound of his voice he stood five, maybe six feet behind her. Were her legs going to buckle? Her heartbeat hitched up. She suddenly felt unsure. She wasn't ready to see him—but he was here.

Removing her hand from the incubator, she slowly turned. Her violet eyes locked on his gray eyes. They were cool. Neither spoke. Their eyes sending the message—*I missed you.*

They stood their ground. Barly's pain of losing her more than two years ago when she returned to the fisherman, swirled between them. The gray eyes wide tracing over her hair, draping slightly over her forehead, was pulled back, the overhead lights sparking off the auburn strands. Her porcelain skin, natural rouged cheeks, the light pink lips—no makeup—only her natural beauty. All was as he remembered.

Maria's lips turned up in a wary smile, her eyes filled with sadness. "Barly, it's good to see you. How have you been?" There. She broke the silence but her eyes remained trained on his face—his thick salt and pepper hair curling around his neck, his cheeks a bit flushed, his lips parted. She had hurt him. She hadn't meant to. He had known little about her. Didn't know until just before she left that she was a Federal Witness, that she was living a lie. She couldn't explain anything. She had to remain cool to his advances.

"You look well, Maria. I'm sorry about your husband." He hesitated, what else could he say? He didn't know her husband. "You're specializing in pediatrics, finishing your residency here. Why did you come back?"

There it was. The question. A question she had asked herself many times. She wasn't sure why she had come back to York. She only knew she had to leave Cortez. There was nothing there for her … only her work, and that could be done anywhere. She had made friends in Maine while she was known as Morgan Grant. Maria Grayson had no friends except for Liz and Manny and they lived on the east coast of Florida. Did the real answer to the question of why she returned to Maine lie in the man facing her?

"There was nothing left for me in Cortez. I'm a doctor and really knew nothing about the sea. Nothing about fishing." She averted her eyes, now calm, in control. "I was happy the months I was here. Although, it seems like a very long time ago." She checked the settings on the baby's incubator. "Stella moved in with me. I'm tending a house about ten minutes from the hospital—"

"I see. How long before you finish your residency?" Barly hadn't closed the gap between them—the five feet, the years, the unsaid words. He remained rooted to the floor.

"About a year. Maybe we can have coffee some time. Catch up." *Oh, why did I say that?*

"Yeah ... sure ... I'll call."

With those words, Barly straightened, a broad smile filled his face this time extending to his eyes. "I think I like the new, old, whatever ... you, the way you are ... now. I'm sure we'll be bumping into each other ... yup, you are definitely gorgeous." He chuckled as he closed the gap planting a kiss on her cheek. "See you around." Turning away, he strode out to check on his patients in the cardiac ward, his white lab coat flapping with each step.

Maria closed her eyes, letting go of the breath trapped in her throat. A thin smile broke across her face as she looked through the incubator glass. "Well, baby girl, all things considered that went well. Nothing to fear. We women can certainly conjure up the worst things. Just you wait until you grow up and you meet the male species. So, woman to woman, do you think I should make the first move ... share that cup of coffee sooner rather than later? I did bring up the subject."

The baby kicked her feet, let out a scream turning her tiny pink face to an angry red, her little arms quivering. "All right, all right, you want to be fed. I get it. And, yes I'll call Barly for that coffee. Now stop your fussing."

Chapter 6

———

BARLY PUSHED DOWN ON the spigot, filling his coffee cup as he glanced around the hospital cafeteria. Maria was sitting in her scrubs off to the side next to a window with a view of the hospital's healing garden, a serene space offering a walk of engraved pavers, a fountain, benches, lush landscaping and pergola for privacy. The flowers were bright with dewdrops. Glancing out at the beauty on the other side of the window, she turned back to reading some papers.

"Damn." He flicked the hot liquid from his fingers, a few drops landing on his blue scrubs. Stuffing his black-rimmed glasses in his pocket, he poured the top inch of coffee into the trashcan next to the coffee service. Looking again, he made his decision.

"Okay if I join you?" he asked striding up to her table.

Maria glanced up. "Sure. Have a seat."

Her voice sent chills up his arm. It was soft, like velvet, just above a whisper. There was no smile, but no sign of annoyance either, Barly noted. "In case you're wondering, this doesn't count as fulfilling your invitation for a cup of coffee." His smile was genuine as he patted the bottom of his cup with a paper napkin. "It's Sunday ... on duty or just—"

"Such is the life of a resident. Have you forgotten? There's no such thing as a weekend, or an eight-hour day, or any difference between night and day for that matter."

"Ah, yes." He leaned back in his chair.

"So why are *you* here?" Her chest rising and falling in quick succession—he had rattled her composure.

"Checking on one of my patients. Inserted an emergency stent yesterday—keeping him one more day." Barly sipped his coffee, his eyes scanning her face. "It's good to see you, Maria. The other day doesn't count—I tracked you down. Although, I was surprised to see you at White Pines Memorial and that you had joined their pediatric team. You picked a specialty?"

"Yes. The more I worked with the children, especially the babies, they became my calling. Fortunately, White Pines had an opening."

"Was it hard to leave Florida?"

Maria looked away, a blank stare. It was late morning and there were only a few people talking in hushed tones—a doctor, a lone visitor, and a mother cradling a baby. "No, it wasn't … hard to leave. When Mac died I—"

"Let me guess. You fled like your story when I first met you— let's see, oh yes, a girl from Washington State, whose parents died—"

"Barly, are you trying to pick a fight? You know … that was my cover story. The story the feds gave me."

She hadn't raised her voice, but her eyes turned dark.

"No, no, sorry. No fighting. Stupid thing to say. I just wondered if the cover story was truer than fiction. Wondering if running away is what you do. Now is not the time, but sometime I'd like to hear about what happened when you returned to Cortez. There's much you're not saying. Your eyes are sad—"

"I just lost my husband. I'm not exactly overjoyed," she snapped.

"Hey, I'm not prying … well, maybe I am."

"Excuse me, I have to go for a run."

"A run?"

"Yes, let off steam. You're making my blood boil."

Barly leaned back, his eyes narrowing as Maria lurched from her chair fumbling with the papers on the table, bending to pick up her pen that bounced on the floor.

Snatching the pen before she did, he stood handing it to her, his lips turning up in an amused smile.

"What's so funny?" She took the pen from his fingers.

"We're making progress. You're blood's boiling. Finally, an honest reaction." Barly lifted her chin so she had to look at him. "I want to find out who you are—the blonde woman with the soft voice who melted my heart, or this lovely auburn-haired lady with violet eyes that stirs my own blood. One thing I do know is that the woman standing in front of me is holding herself together by sheer will. She's tough but she's screaming for help."

"Oh, you've got me all figured out? I'm a victim now? Thanks, but no thanks. I'm doing just fine—"

Simultaneously their pagers sounded an emergency alert. Barly pulled his cell, tapped the emergency number as did Maria. Receiving the same message, their eyes locked.

Church fire. Lightning struck the steeple, shooting down to the altar. Smoke and burn victims. One fatality. You're needed at the scene. Stat!

Slapping his cell phone shut, Barly picked up their empty cups, strode to the trash with Maria on his heels. "Do you know where the church is?" he asked as they shoved through the swinging doors from the cafeteria into a wide hallway.

"No."

"I'll drive. Come on, I'm out back." Taking her hand they ran down the hall, out into the tranquil Sunday morning to drive to a scene of fire, smoke, and death.

Chapter 7

———

THICK BLACK SMOKE SPEWED from charred stained-glass windows on each side of the small, white frame church, scorching the white siding up to the splintered spire. Sirens, blow horns, parishioners mingling with bystanders lining the street shouting to one another, added to the chaotic scene as the sun broke through the storm clouds moving out to sea.

Barly pulled to the curb, stomped on the brake pedal. "This is as close as we can get. Fire and police ahead. The medics are behind us. The crowd will let us through," he shouted to Maria as he scooted out from behind the wheel, both in their blue hospital scrubs. She was already weaving her way to the front entrance where the remaining faithful were being helped down the granite steps by several police officers. A woman in the grip of a policeman, her yellow dress and face streaked with soot, grabbed Maria's arm. "You're a doctor?"

Maria nodded. "Are you all right?"

"Inside. You must hurry. There's a man ... two little children, front pew. He's still in there," the woman cried out collapsing in the policeman's arms.

Maria rushed through the large oak doors of the church feeling Barly's hand on her back. "Here, put this over your nose." He shoved a white handkerchief in her hand as they stumbled down the rows of pews, coughing, fighting through the smoke.

Maria pulled up short. "Did you hear that?"

"Yeah, the organ. Front. Left."

Nearing the organ, she tripped on a fire hose falling to her knees. Barly lifted her to her feet as she shouted, "There he is, the man ... but he's not touching the organ."

Barly squatted down, fingers pressed to the man's neck, checking for a pulse. "He's still alive." He shouted to a fireman wielding the nozzle of a hose, spraying water on the front pews, up the red plush carpet to the altar. "Hey, over here."

Maria knelt, squirming to see behind the organist's bench.

Something moved.

She inched forward under the multilayered keyboard. A little boy, a toddler, cradling a baby, crocodile tears running down his cheeks, peeked out at her.

"Hey, big fella, I'm going to help you. My name is Maria," she whispered, her voice soft. "Give me your hand ... and your baby ... your sister?" Maria, head bent, shoulders hunched so she could sit in the cramped space, held out her hands. She guessed the infant was about two months old, the toddler maybe two years old.

The little boy nodded releasing his hold on his baby.

"Barly, here, come here, a baby ... and a little boy ... hurry." She cried out but in a soft voice so as not to scare the little ones.

The fireman, responding to Barly's call for help, radioed for assistance, shouting into the instrument that a doctor discovered a man. Still alive.

"Wait, I'm coming."

Barly crawled on his belly to Maria. "Well, who do we have here? Hello there, big guy ... it's okay. Take my hand. Come here to me. The nice lady has your baby. That's the big boy. Okay, Maria, let's get these two out of here." His voice low, calm.

Maria held the infant to her chest, pulling the little blanket over the baby's head and over her own mouth breathing soft, moist air onto the baby's face.

"No soot on them," Barly whispered between coughing spasms. "Found this air pocket under the organ. Let's go. Careful of the hoses."

Two medics emerged through the smoke, lifted the man onto the stretcher.

Maria cradled the baby watching Barly hold the toddler his pudgy arms circling Barly's neck ... so tender. The baby started whimpering. Barly turned to Maria, and as he did the little boy turned his head and saw the unconscious man. "Daddy, Daddy."

Squirming against Barly's strong grip, he stretched his little arms out to the man on the stretcher.

Barly sought Maria's eyes. Nodded. So, now they knew who the man was—the children's father.

"What's your daddy's name," Barly asked.

"Daddy." Tommy's big blue eyes gushed tears as he struggled to touch his daddy. Barly glanced at the dad. He was in bad shape, still unconscious clinging to life.

Coughing, the medics disappeared down the center aisle as a beam, flames licking the old wood, fell to their left over several rows of pews.

"Smoke still thick. You with me?" Barly called over his shoulder as he pushed forward through the smoke.

Maria nudged his back. She was with him.

As they emerged from the church, Barly called to a police officer. "We have to get these kids to the hospital. Their father is in that ambulance, just leaving."

"Come on. My squad car," the officer said.

The officer gave Maria a hand guiding her with the baby into the car. Climbing in after Maria, Barly held the toddler to his body, tucking his head under his chin. Tommy stopped squirming, thumb in his mouth. Both doctors had smudges of soot on their faces as well black blotches covering their scrubs from crawling under the organ.

Barly stroked the forehead of the little boy. "What's your name, son?"

"Tommy."

"And your baby? Your sister?"

"Tabatha."

"You're a very brave boy, Tommy."

———

THE AMBULANCE RACED DOWN the road to White Pines, slowing only to navigate a turn. The squad car followed close behind.

"When we pull in" Barly said, "I'll hand Tommy to one of the nurses to help you take these two little ones to Pediatrics. I'll be down in the ER," Barly said, glancing at Maria. She nodded in agreement as she rocked the baby.

The ambulance swung into the hospital's driveway coming to a gentle stop at the emergency entrance, the squad car braking along side.

Each holding a child in their arms, Maria and Barly quickly exited the police car, rushed up to the back of the ambulance as the medics lifted the gurney holding the man out of the vehicle.

"Dr. Bartholomew, the man has a prosthetic leg—down from the knee. We checked his pockets for identification but found nothing. I radioed the firemen to look for his wallet around the organ. They said they would," the medic shouted as he disappeared through the automatic, sliding-glass doors.

Chapter 8

___

MIDNIGHT ROUNDS WERE COMPLETE. Nurses gathered at the Pediatric station, updating charts, when Barly quietly exited the elevator on the second floor. He had showered, shaved, and dressed in a white shirt, open at the neck, and black trousers—trading scrubs for street clothes, and contact lenses for black-rimmed glasses. He asked about Tommy and baby Tabatha and was directed around the corner. Dr. Grayson was with the baby.

The lights were dim. Most of the infants, toddlers, and young children were sleeping, hopefully dreaming of happy places.

Rounding the corner, Barly saw Maria a few yards ahead. She too had showered but redressed in clean scrubs. She was sitting next to an incubator, a precaution he surmised to be sure the baby's lungs were clear of any smoke or soot residue. Maria's hand was inserted into the incubator, a finger resting on Tabatha's tiny hand, the baby's left foot wrapped in a bulky bandage.

Maria was talking softly, so quiet that Barly couldn't make out what she was saying. He didn't need to hear to understand the love Maria was giving the little person—an angel watching over her charge. Maria was calm, relaxed. She was in her element. The passion she felt for her chosen field was evident. A warm loving woman battered by what life had thrown at her.

Another data point for Barly. Bit by little bit a picture of the compassionate lady doctor was emerging. But he wanted … no, he *had* to learn more about her. He fought the instinct to gather her into his arms, whisper in her delicate ear that everything was going to be all right. Of course, he knew better. He feared the walls she erected, walls she thought would protect her from the pain that came from the men she had known, or men who had threatened her.

Feeling his eyes, Maria looked up, her head tilted, an eyebrow raised slightly. Why was he standing there?

Pulling a chair from against the wall, Barly sat beside her, shoving his hands in his pockets so they wouldn't touch her, wouldn't run his hand over her shoulders which he was sure were tired.

"How's she doing? What's with the foot?"

"Seems content. Her little toe was burned or hurt somehow. Bad enough I had to amputate—just to the first knuckle. She'll still be able to wear stilettos." Maria chuckled. Tabatha was awake, her little legs kicking on cue. "Did you ever see such blue eyes? She smiled at me. She trusts me."

"Yeah. What about Tommy?" Barly scanned the cribs, then saw the shock of brown hair two beds down.

"He's sleeping. Poor little guy has been through some tense hours since yesterday." Maria looked back through the glass of the incubator.

"How long will you keep her in there?"

"She should be fine by tomorrow afternoon. Actually, her throat is clear now … I just want to be sure. You're wearing your glasses. Eyes tired? How's the daddy?"

Barly looked down at his hands clasped together, arms resting on his thighs. "He died an hour ago. Too much smoke. His heart failed. When I got in, I found … I couldn't save him."

"Oh, Barly, no. I'm so sorry. We don't even know his name … did the police find his wallet at the church?" Her voice was hopeful until she saw him shake his head. "Anything we can do?"

"I took a picture of him just before he died, and a picture of the prosthetic. There's a number on it. I'd say he's military—head shaved, muscular. Maybe his DNA will—"

"Donovan. Agent Alex Donovan. Maybe he can help unless you have a contact."

"No, I don't. Who's Agent Donovan?"

"The Federal Agent, who shepherded Morgan Grant into existence, paved the way for me to get my license to practice in Maine, responsible for Morgan Grant's history, identity. He will know who to contact, maybe even do it himself. Maybe someone can match the mystery man in the military database."

"Sounds like a plan, Dr. Grayson. It's strange that no one has inquired about the children, or the man. Everyone in the church has been identified. The man is the only fatality. When we got the alert, the message was one dead but that was false. A few others were admitted from the smoke. Two are critical but I think they'll pull through. Others were checked in to the ER and released. One had a sprained ankle the result of a fall trying to escape the fire. Anyway, do you still have this agent's telephone number?"

"Yes. He's sort of my lifeline. These kids must have grandparents. And where's their mother? The man's wife?"

"I don't know. Maybe someone will inquire about the dad later this morning." Leaning in for a closer look at the baby, Barly splayed his hand lightly on Maria's back. His stomach lurched feeling her release a breath, pressing back slightly against his palm, or was it his imagination?

Chapter 9

A PUFF OF GRAY CLOUD SLID over the moon as Maria tiptoed into the house. A weary smile crossed her drawn face—one of the best things she ever did was inviting Stella to live with her. Thanking her for her thoughtfulness—leaving the foyer light on, casting warm shadows, welcoming her home. Jenny, too, was a joy, waiting as she stepped through the door, nudging her hand for a pat.

Kicking off her shoes, Maria padded barefoot to the kitchen to settle her wired nerves with a cup of warm milk. It was not quite twenty-four hours since she had been sipping coffee in the hospital cafeteria, twenty-four hours since tangling with Barly. Yet his sharp words had dimmed, almost forgotten—so much had happened between then and now.

Mulling over the time since the emergency alert, she and Barly had clearly worked in unison at the fire, with the children, and on the same page showing their feelings for the two little kids. And then his touch on her back as they both leaned in to see the tiny soul lying under the glass. Did he feel the same warmth through the palm of his hand as she had?

Pouring the milk into the pan she caught Tabatha's scent on the sleeve of her scrubs. The scent of a baby released a puff of air through her lips drawing to a smile.

"Hey, you, add a little more milk to that pan. Tell me what happened to the baby." Stella in short PJs, mussy hair, yawning, leaned against the counter. Nonetheless, her eyes were wide, waiting to hear the story. "And, by the way, I don't know how you managed to think of me, but thanks for calling that you'd be late. I had surmised as much when I saw you on the evening news—you and Barly climbing into the ambulance." Stella stuck out a mug for her half of the milk.

"She's precious, Stel. Big blue eyes. Her little foot was tinged by the fire. Not bad except for the littlest toe on her left foot. I had to amputate just above the nail. Shouldn't bother her as she grows. She can make up all kinds of stories to tell the boys and, believe me, there will be scads of boys with her blue eyes, plump bow lips, and a sunny disposition unless she's hungry, then she screams bloody murder."

"Wow, all that in a few hours? You practically have her married. You look tired. Can I fix you a sandwich—PBJ on wheat?"

"Sounds good, but I can get it."

"Don't you move a muscle. About time I waited on you for once. The little boy Barly was carrying, how is he?" Stella asked retrieving the apricot jam from the refrigerator.

"He's fine. A little hero taking care of his baby sister. Barly looked comfortable with Tommy. That's his name, according to Tommy. And his baby sister is Tabatha, again according to her almost-two-something big brother. At least, that's how old I think he is. Umm, this should help me sleep. Thanks."

"What about their parents?"

Maria looked up at Stella. "There was a man lying unconscious next to the children. I think he stuffed them under the organ hoping they would be safe and then he must have passed out. The medics put him in the ambulance and drove straight to the ER. Barly tried to save him, but the man's heart gave out. It's awful, Stel. He died. Never regained consciousness. I saw Barly later. I could tell by his face that it affected him deeply. We don't know who the man is. No ID in his pockets. But we do know he's the kids' father. Tommy called him daddy."

"Oh, Maria, that's so sad. The mother?"

"No word from her yet. Everyone seems to be accounted for … except for the man. He was the only one who didn't make it through the fire."

"I guess the police are trying to ID him?"

"Yes, but nothing so far. I'm going to call Agent Donovan. You met him … the day …

"Stop." Stella raised her hand. "Don't remind me of *that* day. Believe me I remember Donovan. He was one of the agents in the kitchen who explained what we were supposed to do to pull off the sting to get that bad guy who was after you. Makes me shudder ... I still can't get the image of the guy filled with bullet holes like a piece of Swiss cheese ... the lying piece of shit ... leading me on the way he did. If I can't forget, I can't imagine how you're coping with it all."

"Now *you* stop. Those things happened to Morgan Grant eons ago. At least that's how I'm coping, compartmentalizing those days, burying them in a locked, steel vault." Maria took a sip of milk and then a bite of peanut butter sandwich. "The man ... little Tommy calling him daddy, brings tears to my eyes. Anyway, the man had a prosthetic leg. We think maybe military and that's why I'm going to enlist Donovan's help. Barly took a picture of the man and his leg before he died. There was a number on the prosthetic. We're hopeful that Donovan will have enough information to learn his identity, plus Barly will send a lock of the man's hair for DNA matching."

Sipping her milk, Maria glanced at Jenny on the rug. She was working on her paw.

Stella followed her gaze. "Jenny and I have a story to tell you, too."

Maria knelt by Jenny turning her paw to see the pad. Jenny winced, pulling away. "Did she step on a pricker?"

"That, dear friend, is our story. A lovely little man, Waldo, came into the shop this afternoon. He was picking up some office supplies—very shy. I offered to help him but he declined, thanking me for *being kind*. Quite a change from how I was treated by that piece of shit, Mr. Swiss cheese. Anyway, Mr. Shy drops a box of thumbtacks, and missy over there trots up to see what the noise was about and steps on two tacks. Yelped and carried on—you'd think her paw was cut off."

"Ouch. Must have hurt. Poor baby," Maria cooed holding Jenny's muzzle, looking into her adoring black eyes, caressing her silky head. The mistress received a thank-you slurp on the cheek.

"Waldo felt awful. And, he insisted I bring her to his clinic. Turns out he's a veterinarian—about a mile out of town. It's no wonder he's a vet—too shy for people, but was best buds with your dog. He cleaned her paw, put on some ointment and a bootie which is probably in the living room somewhere."

"Sounds like Waldo, however shy, is a very kind man."

"Oh, he is. You should have heard him talking so softly to her nibs. I swear Jenny knew exactly what he was saying. I would like a man to talk to me in such sugary tones."

"Maybe you should take *her nibs* in for a post-op consultation and maybe he will."

"I don't know ... well, maybe. I sure wouldn't want Jenny's paw to get infected ... now would I?"

"You said a little man. How little is little?" Maria asked setting her empty mug in the dishwasher.

"I'd say he's the same as me—five feet. I was taller with my heels on. He didn't say much ... to me. But he had a warm smile. I think he wanted to say more. A little tongue tied. That was why he dropped the thumbtacks ... when I asked if I could help. Also, you've been holding out on me."

"And how is that?"

"Oh, just gleaning behind-the-story from the TV reporter at the scene where I saw that yummy Doctor Bartholomew climbing into the squad car after you. I guess he doesn't hold a grudge or decided to let it go."

"Stel, what are saying?"

"His trying to get over you leaving him flat, heart bleeding all over York when you returned to Florida to marry the fisherman."

"Bleeding all over York?"

"Just sayin." Stella hid a smirk as she put her empty milk cup in the dishwasher next to Maria's, and with a wily grin waved goodnight.

Chapter 10

——

DRESSED IN A FRESH PAIR of blue scrubs, Maria walked into the hospital cafeteria for a needed jolt of caffeine. Her steps were not as snappy as usual—went to bed at two o'clock and now it was 6:30. Little sleep, on top of the fire, had taken a toll.

The lead headline in the local morning newspaper caught her attention. Leaning against the counter she read the first paragraph of the story.

Miracle Baby Survives
Lightning Strike on Church Steeple

A baby, cradled by a toddler, was found under the organ keyboard of the church out on the York County line. A summer storm swept in from the west causing power outages. A lightning bolt struck the church spire setting the old white clapboard building on fire. Parishioners exited the church coughing, eyes blurring as they ran through the smoke. An unidentified man was transported to White Pines Memorial Hospital where he died two hours later. He wasn't as lucky as the baby and the toddler who protected her ...

"Good morning." Barly smiled as he handed Maria a mug of steaming hot coffee.

"Thanks, just what I need." Her smile was tired but warm, accepting the mug he extended to her. "Your eyes still burn?"

He looked over the black rims. "Yeah, burning like hell. All that smoke. That's the trouble with contacts."

"Did you see the paper? Lightning definitely caused the fire."

"I did. Have you seen them yet, Tabby and Tommy?" He knew she had. There was a drop of drool on her shoulder.

Maria smiled inwardly with his calling Tabatha, Tabby. Referring to her by the diminutive name—a sign that the baby had tugged on his heart strings as well. "Yes, on my way in. They're sleeping peacefully. They'll wake up to a very different world."

Barly followed Maria to a nearby table. No visitors were chatting this early in the morning. A doctor sat off in the corner drinking a cup of strong, dark roast brew before starting rounds.

Sitting down at the table, folding the newspaper so the article on the fire was on top, Maria pulled her cell from her pocket and tapped an entry in the directory.

"Donovan."

"Good morning, Agent Donovan. It's Dr. Maria Grayson, A-K-A Dr. Morgan Grant," Maria said with a lilt in her voice. "I'm sorry if I woke you. I wanted to be sure to catch you before—"

"Hey, you're selling me short. Of course, I know who you are. Recognized your voice, but your name came up on my phone so I can't take all the credit. And, no, you didn't wake me. I was about to leave for the office. How are you doing? Did I miss something on your history?"

"I'm fine and, no, you didn't miss anything. Thanks again for your help in merging my identities. The White Pines Memorial Hospital hasn't received my original documents from New Orleans, but they accepted my credentials from Florida. I'm finishing my residency here, specializing in Pediatrics. I'm calling on a different matter. I need your help ... *again*."

Maria filled the agent in on what had transpired at the church— two children, and the man who the toddler called Daddy. "I don't think you met Dr. Joe Bartholomew when you were here before ... back when ... anyway, he and I are trying to identify the father. Tommy, he's the little boy, calls the man Daddy." Maria looked up at Barly as she spoke and then back at the newspaper, drawing tiny hearts under the headline.

"What have you got so far?"

"Not much. Nothing in his pockets. But he has a prosthetic leg. There's a number on it. We think he might be military. Dr.

Bartholomew took his picture just after he died. I'll email it to you along with a picture of his leg. I thought maybe—"

"Ask Dr. Bartholomew to send me a sample of his DNA. A clip of his hair. While I wait for the DNA, I'll send the pictures to my contact at Walter Reed here in Washington ... get a trace started. This number good to reach you on?"

"Yes, my cell ... always with me. Any chance you might have something for us today—"

"The FBI is good but not exactly miracle workers. I'll keep you updated."

"Little Tabby already has one miracle to her credit—living through the fire—so why not another. Thanks, Alex. Hold on a minute." Holding the cell away from her ear, Maria tapped Barly's hand drawing his attention from the newspaper. "Did the police get in touch with you? Anyone asking about the man?"

Barly shook his head.

"I guess that's it, Alex. No one's asked about the daddy. Maybe after seeing the story in the paper and probably on TV, someone will come forward, inquire about him. No word from the mother either. She may not be aware of what happened. Please impress upon your contact that this is urgent. We have a baby and a toddler waking up in the hospital with no parents. A scary situation for them."

Chapter 11

San Francisco, California

THE OPULENT STUDY IN the penthouse atop a 1930's style San Francisco building was home base for Susan and Jeffrey Sinclair. The four floors beneath them housed an orphanage—quarters for ten to fifteen children at any given time. The orphanage was a front for the Sinclair's very lucrative black-market baby business.

As was the couple's custom, they relaxed in the mahogany-paneled study—floor-to-ceiling windows, heavily draped, facing the bay, should they have a desire to glance west. Neither spoke, didn't have to. Married for twenty-five some odd years, their brainwaves were always in sync.

They were engrossed in a television news report about a miracle baby surviving a lightning bolt through the spire of a church. The father was dead and there didn't appear to be a mother tending to her infant. The baby was to remain in the hospital for the foreseeable future until relatives were located. The couple spent several hours every week scouring the internet for stories such as this—a baby suddenly orphaned.

"What do you think, Jeffrey?" Susan asked touching the diamond stud in her earlobe, then smoothing a blonde strand of hair in place around her cheek. "Sounds like an opportunity to make a hefty profit. Wouldn't have to pay a surrogate mother. Save us twenty-six, even thirty-eight thousand dollars, and we wouldn't have to wait nine months to collect a hundred grand or more on the sale." She pulled her pedicured toes up under her silk kimono, her eyes narrowing at the prospect of a large profit.

"No wonder I love you so much, my dear. You always know what I'm thinking," Jeffrey said grinning at his wife, his shock of white hair still dewy from his morning shower. He glanced at the gold watch showing beneath his red velvet lounging jacket. "But, we would have to act quickly while the infant is still in the hospital. She's a white baby. What do you think about Diane Thompson? She's been waiting for three months to adopt a baby with us—a year or more at another agency after she lost her husband. Fatal heart attack. So sad. She's at the top of our list. Such a nice woman. Praised your website design—*easy to find, easy to use*—and now, maybe easy to fulfill her dreams. The baby in the clip is adorable, could pass for her own, same blue eyes—maybe worth a premium of another twenty-five thousand don't you think?"

———

"HELLO."

"Cookie?"

"Only with red sprinkles."

"Good. How's Boston?" Susan asked.

"Beautiful."

"We have an assignment for you. However, it's imperative the job be executed within the next forty-eight hours or it's to be aborted, meaning there would be no payment. I presume this is okay with you." Susan rolled her eyes at Jeffrey. Of course it would be okay with Cookie. They paid her well—$25,000 on delivery, so to speak.

"Sounds tricky. Not much time to set up, scout the place. Where is it?"

"York, Maine—not far from you. Have you seen the TV reports today about a miracle baby?" Susan twisted a curl around her finger, waiting for Cookie's reply.

"Yeah. I don't know ... could be difficult. I may not be able to pull it off. Let's say it works, where will you accept the package?"

"Here, at the orphanage. Jeffrey will call you in the next thirty minutes with the details."

Chapter 12

———

Boston, Massachusetts

A TERRORISM CONFERENCE HOSTED by Boston's prestigious Marriot Hotel on Long Wharf, one block from Faneuil Hall and Quincy Market, was sponsored by Rudy Giuliani, former mayor of New York City, and his counter-terrorism group. The oversubscribed conference was off to a fast start with a packed first-morning session. When the speaker wrapped up for the lunch break, the attendees scattered for a much needed stretching of their legs. Two private detectives dressed alike—black shirt, black trousers, sturdy black leather shoes for him, sassy black heels for her—sauntered arm-in-arm to the lobby.

"I don't know about you, husband of mine, but I could sure use a cold drink," Liz said, sinking onto a couch filled with pillows, her mop of red curls sparking attention from other attendees passing by. "Do we have time to walk to Quincy Market, have lunch, and get back for the afternoon ... Manny, look at the TV. It's Maria ... getting into that police car. She has a baby in her arms ... listen ... what's the reporter saying ...

"Yesterday, a baby survived a lightning bolt through the spire of a church on the outskirts of York, Maine. The father is dead and the whereabouts of the mother is unknown. Doctors Maria Grayson and Joe Bartholomew found the baby and her little brother under the church's organ."

"Stitch, what are you doing?"

"Calling Maria. Looks like she's a—"

"Liz, is that you?" Maria held her cell to her ear as she adjusted a setting on Tabatha's incubator.

"Hey, girlfriend, you're famous. Manny and I are at a conference in Boston and there you are on the television. Is that baby okay?"

"Yes. I have her in an incubator but she'll be in a crib tomorrow, maybe even tonight. I want to make sure her little lungs are clear. You and Manny are at a conference in Boston, you said? Can you come up? York is ... you know where it is. You were here ... you know."

"Yeah, straight up the 95 Interstate. What, about a two-hour drive?"

"Under two. Can you make it?"

"Of course, we can make it. You were already on our itinerary. I was going to call you as soon as we knew how this conference was going to play out—there'll be some sort of get-together after the last class. Smoozing. Blah blah blah. Hang on. What did you say, Manny? ... yes, we'll drive up after the last session—where?"

"My house. Tons of room so you have to stay with me. I have a roommate, Stella. You met her ... you know ... Do you have a pen?"

"Never without. The conference lasts two more days. I'll text you with our ETA. Promise you won't fuss?"

"I promise, but a little extra wine ... for old time's sake."

Chapter 13

Cary, North Carolina

AN AGENT WITH THE FBI for twenty-five years, Donovan had a deep respect for the missions the U.S. military carried out every day. The thought that maybe a serviceman was killed by a bolt of lightning leaving two infant children tugged at his heart. Others in the bureau were of a like mind and joined Donovan, pulling out all the stops to find the identity of the man Dr. Maria Grayson was searching for. By morning a tentative ID of the man had been made, waiting only for confirmation of his DNA. The lock of the man's hair was due to arrive at their labs later in the day.

Donovan, even without the lock of hair, knew in his gut that the man was Army Staff Sergeant Steven Caldwell from Cary, North Carolina, a small town just outside of Raleigh.

This was not going to be a pleasant assignment, but Donovan urged the Raleigh office to dispatch an agent as soon as possible—a two-month-old baby and a toddler were homeless, orphans. Per Donovan's orders, Agent Phillips was sent from the Raleigh Bureau, the picture Dr. Bartholomew had taken tucked in his pocket for positive identification, and, if corroborated, to notify the parents of their son's death.

Donovan also texted Maria that he was fairly certain they had found the children's grandparents. He would call in a couple of hours if the Caldwells confirmed that the man in the picture was indeed their son.

AGENT PHILLIPS, BLACK SUIT, white shirt, black and white striped tie, strode up the short flagstone walkway lined with pink petunias to the small white clapboard house. Pots of geraniums flanked the front door. Mounting the four steps, hesitating a moment, then with a quick breath he pushed the doorbell.

A diminutive silver-haired woman opened the door wiping her hands on a daisy-flowered apron. Judging from the supposed age of the dead man, thirty something, the woman looked to be in her early to mid-sixties, falling in the age range of the sergeant's mother.

"Who is it, Sylvia?" The deep gravelly voice came from a room off the small foyer.

"Wait, Steven." Sylvia looked through the screen at the man with soft brown eyes standing at attention on the other side. A warm smile spread across her face, relieved the man wasn't in uniform or, for sure, he could be bearing bad news concerning her son who was in the Army. "Can I help you, sir?" Her voice was sweet like her apple cheeks.

"Are you Mrs. Caldwell?"

"Yes."

"My name is Agent Phillips. I'm with the FBI and looking for a Mr. and Mrs. Steven Caldwell." Phillips forced a thin smile showing the woman his badge. "I came to ask you about your son."

"Oh, dear, is Stevie in trouble?"

"May I speak with you and your husband?"

"I suppose so. Yes, yes, come in. Steven, an FBI agent is here to talk to us," Sylvia called out. She led the way into the living room and introduced Agent Phillips to her husband.

"Please, have a seat," Mr. Caldwell said. "I heard you inquiring about our son. He's not here. What is it you want to know about Stevie?"

"Well … first, do you know where your son was on Sunday?"

"He told us he'd be traveling. Didn't say where," Sylvia said. "He's on leave."

"Does he have a prosthetic leg?"

"Yes, he does. He was injured in Afghanistan. Amazing how he's able to get around, isn't it Steven. But, you sound like you already know this."

"Do you have two grandchildren, Mrs. Caldwell?"

"One for sure. A baby girl. Her name is Tabatha."

"Does she have a brother ... Tommy?"

"That's a long story. Please, Agent Phillips, tell us why you're here. Is Stevie in trouble?" Sylvia's eyes widened, her fingers squeezing the daisy apron.

"There was a storm on Sunday ... up north. A bolt of lightning struck a church spire—York, Maine. A man was injured from a fire caused by the lightning. A doctor operated but the man had a bad heart and died a few hours later." Phillips pulled out a print of the picture Barly had taken and handed it to Mr. Caldwell. "Is this your son, sir?"

Steven Caldwell took the picture. Clutched his heart. Closing his eyes, his hand shaking, he passed the picture to his wife.

"Oh, no ... not my Stevie." Dropping the picture to her apron, tears spilling down her cheeks, she pulled a white hanky trimmed in lace from her apron pocket. Breathing heavily, she rubbed her tear-filled eyes hard. Gasping for air, her red eyes peeked over the hanky at the agent. "Baby Tabatha, where is she?"

"She's okay, ma'am. She's being cared for at White Pines Memorial Hospital along with Tommy. What about your son's wife? She didn't seem to be with him and hasn't inquired at the hospital."

"Stevie was ... actually, he was trying to find her. Steven, we have to go to Maine. We have to see Tabatha. Agent Phillips, where's our son?"

"His body was transferred by the York Coroner to the morgue."

Both Caldwells shuddered at the agent's words.

Sylvia blew her nose, trying to regain her composure. "Agent Phillips, will you help us make reservations? We'll fly as soon as we can but we don't know exactly how, or where, or ... please, can you help us?"

Chapter 14

York, Maine

MARIA SETTLED BABY TABATHA in the hospital bassinet. Her lungs had cleared so she no longer needed the controlled air of the incubator. Tucking the pink receiving blanket up to the baby's little chin, Maria retrieved the vibrating cell from her pocket. "Alex, any word?"

"Yes. The man you found is Staff Sergeant Steven Caldwell, North Carolina. Caldwell's records indicate that he's ….was at the beginning of a two-month leave. We still want to confirm the DNA but our agent from the Raleigh office just called. He visited the man's parents and they identified the man in the picture as their son. The agent is helping them with arrangements to fly to Portland, Maine, and then rent a car to drive to York, if they're able. They're pretty shaken, as you might guess, and the grandfather doesn't seem well. I don't know what his health issues are. I'd say they should arrive in a couple of days."

"I bet they're concerned, worried about their grandchildren."

"Yes and not so much. I don't know what the story is. They talked about their granddaughter Tabatha but seemed to be, I don't know, estranged from the boy. They refused to say anything about his wife except that he was traveling to her, or trying to find her. Our agent wasn't able to learn anymore. They didn't seem to know much about the wife's family and the agent said they weren't in any shape to press them."

Barly entered the ward to check on Tommy. Seeing Maria was on the phone he touched her arm as he passed to the sleeping little boy's crib. Hearing Maria sign off, he turned to find a big smile—a full-face smile. Now this was more like the woman he had been with three years ago.

Maria motioned for him to follow her out the door. She was bursting with news and, from the expression on her face, it was all good.

The door swinging closed behind them, she abruptly stopped in her tracks, her hand grasping Barly's wrist.

"They've identified the man. Steven Caldwell, Army. And, not only that, they found the grandparents in North Carolina, and they're coming to get the children, or at least they're coming. Maybe in two days. Isn't that great? I tell you, that Agent Donovan knows how to do a job."

"You're babbling." Barly casually put his arm around her shoulders as they headed to the cafeteria. Coffee'd out by the end of the afternoon, they both had started a habit of sharing a cup of tea if he was in the hospital.

"What do you mean I'm babbling? It's such good news. Alex found everyone so quickly, and—"

"Whoa. See what I mean—babbling. Morgan never babbled and I think I know why."

"And what do you know, Agent Bartholomew?"

"Morgan never relaxed. Morgan was always scared as to who would pop out around the next corner. But, Maria ... well ...

"Maria, well what?"

"There you go again—a full-face smile—very nice relaxed shoulders, a grin, even playful and brimming with information that you're *sharing* with me ... real information. Not made up."

Maria smiled up at him, punched his arm, shaking her head, dramatically furrowing her brows, mocking his words.

"Yup, I think I'm beginning to warm up to this woman."

"Beginning?" Feigned shock gripped her face.

Suddenly, his teasing stopped, he looked away. "Yes, *beginning* ... but today I'll call it progress." Barly stepped back in the wide hallway, a gurney transporting a patient hooked to a drip bag pushed by, followed by a food cart. Barly gently placed his hand on Maria's arm. "You can trust me, Maria. Don't fade from me, don't put up walls. I couldn't—"

Maria put her index finger on his lips. "Don't say any more, Barly. I'm Maria. Let's just keep moving forward, enjoy the moment, neither one of us thinking too far ahead until we come to a turning point ... good or bad." Barly's fingers tightened on her arm. He ached to kiss her right there in the hall with the dinner service trolleys clanging by.

"So, Dr. Bartholomew, are you going to put a teabag in a mug of hot water for me or not? We have some planning to do."

"Planning?"

"Yes. Tommy and Tabby need a new wardrobe if they're going to be reunited with their grandparents."

Chapter 15

A YOUNG WOMAN WEARING a yellow tank-top over white slacks and a black tote over her shoulder, entered the hospital. Her brunette hair curled from under a Red Sox ball cap, the bill pulled down to her brows. She followed close behind two men and a young girl, wearing jeans topped with various colored T-shirts. The two men were in a heated discussion when the brunette breezed by the girl and the men, to the information desk.

"Excuse me. Can you direct me to the pediatric floor?"

"Certainly, dear." The seventyish volunteer lady leaned across the desk opening a map. "You're standing here, dear." She marked an *X* on the map with a thick black pen. Picking up another pen with a smaller point, she continued giving directions drawing a line to the elevators. "See here, turn to your right, down the hall to the elevator. Pediatrics is on the second floor." The lady peered over her glasses, brows raised, questioning if the young woman understood.

"Thank you." The brunette looked down, picked up the map, and walked briskly to the elevator. At the second floor, exiting the elevator, she jumped out of the way as a cart flashed by pushed by a male attendant. A nurse wearing green scrubs walked behind the cart carrying a clipboard, her finger scanning down a list of some sort.

The brunette followed the nurse to a door marked STAFF. The nurse disappeared inside the STAFF room. Outside the door was a bin. The STAFF door swung open and a large man dressed in street clothes rushed to the elevator dropping a set of scrubs in the bin as he passed. The brunette paid attention to everyone, and to everything they did, and whether anyone paid any attention to her. Walking around the nurses' station she saw something of interest, something that could be useful, could cause chaos—a fire alarm box.

A baby cried in the distance. The brunette slowly walked toward the sound of the baby. A young man in scrubs carrying a tray of bottles started to walk by but the brunette stepped in front of him. "Excuse me. I'm looking for my sister. She said she would be with baby Tabatha, the baby who survived—"

"Next door on your right. Can't miss the baby. She's in a crib with a pink bow on the side. Her names on the top."

The brunette strolled to the door, glanced left and right, and entered the room. She saw the crib with the pink bow, saw a sleeping infant, and then saw the name tag—Tabatha. She looked around the crib-filled room and then began to retrace her steps. Walking to the STAFF door, she scanned the hallway. Seeing no one, she snatched the discarded blue scrubs from the bin, quickly pushed them into her tote, and stepped into the elevator in front of two nurses snickering over an encounter with a hottie male intern.

At two o'clock that night, a very pregnant woman in blue scrubs stepped off the elevator on the second floor. Her heart pounding, she walked quickly down the empty hall. No one at the nurses' station, she glanced away from the fire alarm box and walked around the corner stepping into the dimly lit ward and to baby Tabatha's bassinet. Picking up the baby, cradling the infant in her arms, she walked down the hall to the sign REST ROOM. In the restroom, she discarded her baby bump and carefully positioned the infant in a harness pulling the large scrub top down over her very protruding tummy.

Leaving the rest room, the pregnant employee rode the empty elevator to the first floor, hustled passed the unattended information desk and out of the front door. She quickly walked to her car, opened the back door, leaned in, and with some difficulty removed the baby whose face was turning red and about to let out a scream. She settled the baby into an infant car seat, stroked her lips with a pacifier, coated with a sedative. The baby eagerly sucked the pacifier, her red face returning to a nice pink.

Driving out of the parking lot and down two blocks to a secluded area with tall oaks blocking the street light, the brunette jumped out of the car, doffed the scrubs covering her jeans and black T-shirt into a bag, along with the Red Sox ball cap and a brunette wig. Quickly sliding back into the car, she drove the short distance to Interstate 95, turning onto the ramp south to Boston.

Passing the 24-hour car rental office an hour later, the non-pregnant woman continued for two blocks, pulling into a strip-mall lit only by a blinking neon sign, Mattress Heaven, and parked in the slot next to a gray Toyota.

She then transferred her precious cargo together with the bag of scrubs, cap and wig, into the back seat of the Toyota—her car. Cracking the window so the baby would have a little fresh air, she locked the door, smoothed her blonde hair and drove the rental car back to the agency. Within minutes she pulled into the 24-hour car rental office. Inside, she dropped the car keys on the counter startling the sleepy attendant.

"Hey, doll face, what's your hurry? It's a slow night, how about coming with me to take that car behind the lot." He yawned taking an appraising gander tip to toe of the blonde standing in front of him.

"No thanks. I'm in a bit of a hurry."

"Hey, come on. Anyway, I have to check the car. Make sure you didn't ding it up."

"All right. But then I have to be on my way. My bruiser of a boyfriend is waiting for me."

"Yeah, sure." The scrawny attendant checked the mileage then nonchalantly walked around the car, made a note on his clipboard, and handed her the invoice. "Okay, Blondie, if you don't want to have a little drink out back, I guess that does it."

Paying the bill in cash, the blonde left the rental agency, her feet hurriedly tapping the sidewalk as she disappeared down the dark street. A shiver raised the hairs on her arm as she darted the two blocks back to her car, clutching her purse to her chest, breathing in short gasps. She never ventured out at night unless it was absolutely necessary and never on dark streets, streets in areas of the city ripe with crime—addicts always needing cash for their next fix.

She heard laughter from some bushes as she walked by. Her step quickened to a trot surmising the noise came from kids getting high on crack.

Breaking into a fast jog, she rounded the corner to her car. Fumbling with her keys, her hand shaking, she pressed the button, dropped the keys, her nails scraping them up off the pavement. She pressed the button on the keychain again and the latch clicked open. Throwing her purse on the front seat of the passenger side, she nervously slid behind the wheel, slammed the door, and took off out of the strip mall to Boston's Logan Airport, a fifteen minute drive. Earlier she had clocked the distance from where she planned to park the car at the airport to be sure of her timing.

Approaching the brightly lit streets leading to the airport, her breathing eased. Her heart returned to its normal rhythm. Smiling, she glanced in the rearview mirror at the baby.

Baby?

Her body froze.

The car seat was empty.

Chapter 16

SIPPING HER EARLY MORNING coffee, Maria stared out the hospital's cafeteria window—gray turning to dawn. Yesterday's spring had morphed into an early summer wave of heat and humidity.

For the last several nights since the fire, since holding baby Tabatha in her arms, since looking into little Tommy's big blue eyes, she had dreamed the children were hers. Living with her—the picture of a happy family. The missing piece was a father figure, missing in her dreams. She'd have to hire a nanny. Certainly the house was big enough. Strange how she thought the house was too big when she signed the rental agreement. Maybe she was following destiny's path. Fate?

A squirrel, commanding her attention, sat on his haunches in the middle of a grassy patch. He was looking straight at her as he nibbled on an acorn held in his tiny paws, chewing rapidly. Maria shook her head, knocking out the crazy thoughts pinging through her brain. What if the grandparents didn't want the children, or were not able to care for them. Donovan said that Mr. Caldwell had some health issues but he didn't know what. Yet, they *were* coming to Maine, so how bad could the grandfather's health be?

"Good morning. Penny for your thoughts?" Barly smiled along with a gentle placing of his hand on her shoulder in greeting. An intimate gesture but not so intimate that he couldn't walk away from her.

"Hi. I was thinking, wondering what the Caldwells will do when they see the children. Tabby and Tommy are so cute. They'll melt their grandparent's hearts for sure. But we don't know if they will be able to care for such young children, after all they—"

"You're getting ahead of yourself young lady. In any event you'll know soon enough. Did you hear from Donovan last night? When the Caldwells will arrive?"

"Tomorrow. A neighbor is coming with them as their chauffeur I guess. They're flying into Portland instead of Boston. I don't know what time. Want to come upstairs to say good morning to Tabby and Tommy—the double Ts?" Maria smiled. The pinging hadn't entirely left her mind but she had tamped it down, anxious to give Tabby her morning bottle. The nurses knew her routine and held off feeding the baby unless Dr. Grayson informed them that she was busy with a patient.

"I'm scheduled in the OR in forty-five minutes so I have time to give the little guy a hug." Barly stood, waiting to pull out Maria's chair while she gathered her shoulder bag and laptop.

Strolling out of the cafeteria, they rode the elevator to the second floor. Maria quickened her step as she entered the ward walking straight to Tabby's crib.

Tabby wasn't there.

Maria glanced around for a nurse. It was time for a shift change. Her eyes moved to Barly talking to Tommy. She stepped to his side.

"Good morning, big guy," she said softly to Tommy who was doing a number on his thumb, clutching his Teddy bear, a bear that Barly had given him. Maria looked up at Barly. "I'm going to the nurses' station. One of them must have Tabby. She's probably crying for her bottle. I'll be right back," she said, stroking Tommy's shock of soft brown hair. The toddler fastened his eyes on Maria. "Hey, sweetie, is that a tear I see? Do you have a tummy ache?"

Tommy shook his head, struggled to stand against the side of his crib, put his arms out to Barly. Tommy wanted to be picked up. "I think he's unhappy because he can't see Tabby," Barly said holding the little guy to his chest, patting his back. "I'll go with you."

Several nurses were chatting—those finishing the night shift, going over the charts with those arriving. None were holding Tabby. Maria checked her watch. It was almost six. "Excuse me, Julie, where's Tabby? She's not in her crib."

"I changed her about two this morning. Let me take a look." Julie punched up Tabby's record on the computer. No entry except her own indicating she had checked the baby at 1:35 a.m. Julie looked up to Maria and Barly. Alarm began to spread across her face. "Anyone take Tabby for a procedure, a test, anything after two?" she asked the nurses who had finished their shift.

The nurses shook their heads as Maria snatched the desk phone's receiver, punched the security guard button. Her heart racing, eyes flashing to Barly holding Tommy, who was crying for Tabby.

"Security, Officer Tracy. Can I help you?"

"This is Dr. Grayson, Pediatrics. A baby is missing. She hasn't been seen since two o'clock. Can you put out a page for whoever has baby Tabatha Caldwell to bring her to Pediatrics, or anyone who knows where she is to call the Pediatric nurses' station?"

"Yes. We'll put out the page and I'll be right up, Dr. Grayson. One of our officers will start checking the security camera files."

Maria put the receiver back in the cradle at the same time her cell vibrated. It was Liz.

"Hi, girlfriend. Just wanted to keep you posted. We'll be coming up day after tomorrow for the weekend. Maria … Maria … hey, something wrong?"

"The baby, the baby is missing."

"Scratch what I just said. We're on our way … less than two hours you said?"

"Yes."

"You're where … at the hospital?"

"Yes, White Pines Memorial. Thanks." Maria disconnected the call her eyes peeled on the elevator door sliding open.

Officer Tracy strode off the elevator to the group collected at the Pediatric nurses' station. Maria could see from the expression on his face that no one had answered his page.

Barly took Tommy back to his crib, quickly returning to Maria's side. Concern written on his face, torn between staying with her and knowing he couldn't. He told her he'd see her as soon as he finished the surgery.

Chapter 17

OFFICER TRACY IMMEDIATELY SET up a hospital security team to scrutinize all digital camera files taken between the time the nurse logged her last check of Tabatha to when Dr. Grayson alerted security that the baby was missing. Nothing appeared out of the ordinary.

A pregnant staff member was seen entering the hospital at 2:10 a.m. The same woman was seen leaving at 2:27 a.m. With a print out of the frame showing the woman, Security was in the process of identifying the woman in blue scrubs, but she never faced the camera. A profile was captured of her leaving the hospital, but so far no one recognized her. To facilitate the widening of the search, several prints were made of the frames showing the activity in question.

Human Resources opened their office at 8:30 a.m. Tracy asked if anyone in the office could identify the scrubs-woman. No one could. But a manager, noting the size of the baby bump, said that no one on staff was on the verge of giving birth. The closest was a pregnant nurse who was four months away from delivering her baby.

Tracy placed a call to the York police at 8:55 a.m. notifying them that a baby appeared to have been kidnapped sometime during the early morning hours between two and six-thirty. A possible suspect was caught on camera.

A picture of the infant Maria had snapped the day before was sent to police headquarters.

Chapter 18

———

"COOKIE, WHERE THE HELL are you? Jeffrey and I are waiting at the gate but the pilot and flight crew just passed us. They said everyone had left the plane."

"Susan … Susan … I don't know what to say."

"Stop blubbering, Cookie. I can't understand you. WHERE are you?"

"Boston."

"Boston? Did you miss your flight? Stupid question. Why did you miss your flight?" Susan's eyes narrowed, darting to Jeffrey, her voice near a shriek.

"The baby … I locked the doors of my car … had to return the rental …"

"Okay, SO you locked your car?" The heel of Susan's furry mule slipper was pounding the floor.

"When I got back to my car she wasn't there?"

"What do you mean she wasn't there?" Susan screamed.

Cookie was now sobbing hysterically into the receiver.

"The baby … she was gone."

Chapter 19

———

THE HUNT FOR BABY Tabatha, for someone who could identify the pregnant woman in blue scrubs seen leaving the hospital in the early morning hours, or for *anyone* seen with the baby, was in high gear. York police officers combed the hospital grounds for any kind of clue as to who took the baby, while others meticulously searched through every inch of the hospital starting with the empty crib on the second floor.

An officer exited the ladies restroom on the Pediatric floor with a wad of crumpled newspapers he found in a black trash bag along with a discarded pillow and pillowcase. Laundry bins were checked and released to the cleaning service.

Maria handed Tabby's chart back to the attendant at the nurses' station for the third time. She felt she was missing something but nothing jumped out at her. Hearing her page, she called the information desk and was told an Elizabeth Stitchway, along with a Manny Salinas, were here to see her.

Liz rushed up to Maria as she exited the elevator. The two women hugged, and then it was Manny's turn.

"Maria, tell us what happened. Show us where the baby was last seen," Manny said.

Maria's face was drawn as she grasped Liz's hand. "Come on. I'll take you up to the second floor, Pediatrics." Riding the elevator Maria filled them in on all she knew, which according to Tabby's chart, was precious little. Entering the room of cribs, she led the two PIs to the empty crib with the pink bow. "Sometime between 2:00 a.m. and 6:30 the baby vanished from this crib."

"Who's leading the investigation," Manny asked.

"When I realized something was very wrong, I called hospital security about a baby missing—spoke with Officer Tracy. Shortly after that, he alerted the York police and I think they have taken control of the search. This all happened between when I called you and now—two hours I guess. I'll introduce you to Tracy and—"

Maria glanced over at Tommy standing in his crib holding his blanket to his face, thumb in his mouth staring at her. "Oh, wait a minute. You have to meet Tommy. Tabby's big brother. He was holding her when I found them under the church organ. Hi, there big guy." Maria lifted him from the crib holding his head to hers, smoothing his soft brown hair. "This is Liz and Manny. They're friends, Tommy."

Tommy peered over Maria's shoulder at the two strangers but clung tight to her neck. He was not going to let any strangers hold him.

"Hi, Tommy. You're a hero, big fella. What a good boy you are." Liz gently ran her fingers down his arm.

"My name is Manny. Kinda like Tommy." Manny chuckled, smiling at the toddler. "Did you see your baby sister last night?"

Tommy clutched Maria's neck tighter with his little arm, sucking his thumb harder, his eyes staring at the man's face.

Maria kissed Tommy's head, gently loosening his grip from around her neck, returning him to his crib. Grasping Liz and Manny's hands she led them out of the ward. "I'll take you to Officer Tracy. He'll know who's leading the police. I explained to him that you were coming, two of the best PI's I know—"

"Unless you're holding out on me, we're the only PI's you know," Liz grinned.

Maria smiled. "Doesn't matter—you're still the best." Looking down, drawing an imaginary circle on the floor. "I guess I don't have to tell you I'm scared." Taking a deep breath, she pushed the elevator button. "I talked to Stella, my housemate. I told her that you'll be arriving sometime today. Here's a spare key if no one's there. You have my cell. Please keep me posted."

"We will, Maria," Liz said. Exiting the elevator, Liz grabbed Maria's hand as they walked to the lobby.

Barly rushed in through the glass doors, ignoring the PIs, he hugged her, leaned back. "I called as soon as I could ... have they found her?"

"No," she whispered.

His hands remained on her arms, forcing her eyes to his. "I have some news from Chief Roth. They found Caldwell's wallet in a car in the church parking lot. They didn't notice the car had been left until late yesterday. Some of the people attending church, caught in the fire didn't return for their cars right away, so it wasn't obvious that his was abandoned. His wallet was in a jacket on the floor of the backseat along with some baby stuff and a box of Cheerios."

"So, that's how he arrived at the church ... a piece of good news ... but Tabby—" Maria looked away at Liz turning from Barly's grip.

"Barly, I'd like you to meet two wonderful people who have come to help us, Manny and Liz—"

"Ah, the private investigators. Maria has told me so much about you," Barly said pumping Manny's hand and a quick peck on Liz's cheek. "I hope we can spend some time together ... I'm sorry I have another surgery and I want to see Tommy, but I'm running late ... "

"Go, go. Tommy's adorable. We'll keep you updated." Liz was grinning ear to ear raising her brows at Maria.

"Right. Maria, I'll call you as soon as I can. I've canceled the rest of my appointments but I have this surgery. Leave word if they find Tabby."

Barly waved goodbye as he walked quickly to the elevator.

"So, girlfriend, we have some catching up to do. You haven't exactly told me everything. That's one hunk of manhood that just breezed through here."

"Yes, well, back to business," Manny said. "Liz and I batted around some ideas while driving up here,"

"Tell me." Maria shot a stop-it look at Liz as she pretended to smooth down the top of her scrubs.

Liz snickered at Maria's discomfort, loving how unsettled she was as the breezy man whisked in, squeezed, and whisked out. "We saw you on a cable news report ... that's when I called. Manny and I think, given the news coverage of the miracle baby, that obviously tons of other people will have seen it, say, a wacko wanna-be mother—"

Manny interrupted his wife, "Or, another scenario, someone taking advantage of the fact that the father is dead and no mother around, that it was an opportunity to snatch the baby and sell her. We learned yesterday at one of the sessions that there's been an uptick in baby trafficking."

"Oh, my God, that's terrible," Maria rubbed her fingers up and down her arm. "I did have the thought of a possible wacko—"

"Maria, we didn't want to scare you, but we say it like it is. The good news is, in either of those two possibilities, they would not harm the baby. She represents a lot to them—love or money. Also, Manny and I noted the numerous security cameras inside the entrance to this building as well as the parking lot." Liz lifted Maria's hand, encircling the delicate hand with both of hers in support. "We're going to find the baby."

———

LIZ AND MANNY HUDDLED with the York Police, Chief Keith Roth and Officer Tracy in the hospital's conference room. The one clue they had, but both men knew it to be key, was the surveillance video. The only unidentified person during the hours of two and six, entering or leaving the front entrance, was a pregnant woman in scrubs. The chief felt sure that the woman on the tape had perpetrated the abduction concealing the baby under her scrubs. Tracy picked up the black bag found in a waste receptacle showing them the newspaper and pillow. Maybe it meant something, or maybe it didn't. But at the moment, it was the only lead they had.

Manny looked at Liz and then turned to Chief Roth and Officer Tracy. "Liz and I have been private investigators for several years in the central Florida area. The only reason we were able to get here so fast after we spoke with Dr. Grayson, is because we were attending a conference on terrorism in—"

"You were there? With Giuliani?" Chief Roth asked bug eyed.

"Yeah, you heard about it?" Liz asked grinning.

"You bet I did. The only reason I wasn't there is because I was running some drills with my men—beginning of tourist season you know—so I couldn't get away."

Grinning in return, Manny finished what he was saying. "I just wanted to assure you that Ms. Stitchway and I will not get in your way, and if we come up with anything we'll share it with you immediately."

"Hell, I'm happy to have you. As I said, the tourists are flooding in and we are up to our ears with calls. Great on the sharing and that goes both ways. Let's find this baby."

The huddle broke up, the chief hustling out to his squad car, and Tracy running the security tape of the unidentified pregnant woman for Manny and Liz.

While Manny retraced the officer's steps in and out of the hospital looking for clues, Liz spoke with the night nurse. What was the baby wearing? What was she bundled in, asking the nurse for a similar blanket. After questioning her, Liz talked with Maria in the hallway next to the elevators.

Maria looked to her friend for answers but it was too early to expect anything substantive. There was no smile on her face, brow slightly furrowed, arms crossed as if holding the missing infant to her. She had become attached to the baby, constantly visualizing the minute she pulled her from under the church organ, smoke creeping into the children's cave, initial puffs of smoke entering the baby's lungs with each breath.

"Liz, Tabby has a partial little toe, left foot. Somehow, maybe even from the lightning strike, it was burned. Almost severed. I amputated above the nail, below the first joint. It was healing nicely, no seepage. So, unless whoever has her is very careless, it's healed over enough that it shouldn't become infected."

"Maria, that's key. Thank God you said something. It will help us eliminate crank calls, extortionists, blackmailers even. We'll do the best we can to recover the baby. You said the grandparents are on their way. Do they know she's missing?" Liz said pushing the button for the elevator.

"Not yet, I've been struggling with whether to tell them or not. They just lost their son … maybe you'll find her before they arrive. They're not due until tomorrow."

"I'll keep you posted but these cases can take time. I doubt we'd have anything that quick. We learned the hospital has plans to update their security. That's great, but no help for today. Steel yourself … you're going to have to tell them."

Maria kissed her cheek as the elevator door opened. "Good luck." She watched Liz disappear as the elevator door slid shut. Feeling a hand on her elbow, she jerked away, turned, and let out a gasp of air. "Barly, you startled me. I was just—"

"I know. Same for me … where is she? Praying they find her quickly. My patient's surgery has been rescheduled so I checked with the floor nurse. Two more hours until your shift ends. A Resident doctor is due early. After bringing him up to speed on your little charges, I think you need to leave here, get away. I made sure Officer Tracy and Chief Roth have both of our cell numbers. You're going to let me pamper you a bit while we talk. I'll pick up some extra groceries. Dinner at my place okay?"

Maria didn't hesitate. "I'd like that."

Chapter 20

———

AT FIRST LOOK, it was a modest white cape with black shutters. Modest? Not really.

Barly turned his green Jeep into the driveway, parking in front of the first of three garage doors lined up on the right side of the house. To the left of the main house was an addition that Maria thought to be an apartment with a single-car garage on the end. The house, all added together, equaled an estate nestled in a forest of oak and maple trees.

The first garage door next to the house rolled up as Barly turned off the engine. "It's easier to haul groceries into the kitchen if I leave the car in the driveway." A matter-of-fact statement of habit—a small glimpse into the man, promising more.

Getting out of the Jeep, Barly grabbed some grocery bags from the back seat. "I like your friends," he said handing her two of the bags, celery poking out of the top of one.

"How do you know? You shook hands with Manny and gave Liz a quick peck on the cheek."

"The way they sized me up. More than a detective's instinct, they were checking me out … was I going to hurt you. They were the first glimpse I've had of your life before Morgan. I'm just saying, I liked what I saw."

"Maybe you should be a detective." Her eyes were warm, smiling back at him.

"We doctors *are* detectives, Maria. Not for bad guys but determining what's causing our patient's pain. Of course, your PIs didn't see what you did to me."

Averting his eyes, and his words, she stepped into the garage. Yes, she had hurt him and now he was wary of her. Well, time would tell what fate had in store for them, but for now, at his house, it was her turn to learn more about him.

She peeked through the garage's three bays—separated by doors on the outside, open one to the other inside. "I see you have your toys—riding lawnmower, a boat trailer with a boat on top, and your Mercedes."

"A gardener takes care of the yard, and I use the trailer to haul that small outboard to nearby rivers and to Moosehead Lake."

"Ah, yes. The lake! Do you rent out the addition on the other side of the house? I'd call it an in-law apartment but, unless you're keeping something from me, you don't have any in-laws."

"That's kind of a long story. I'll show you around after I have dinner on the stove and a glass of wine in our hands. Hope you're up for some homemade spaghetti. But, I have one request."

"And that is?"

"No shoptalk until after dinner—hospital or the kids. Then we'll talk. Okay?"

"Actually, that sounds better than okay."

Entering from the garage to the kitchen, each carried a couple of brown grocery bags. Maria set her bags on the black granite island, her eyes scanning Barly's private world. This was definitely a man's kitchen. A six-burner gas stove with a grill element on top of a stainless steel oven was meant for some serious cooking. Shiny aluminum and burnished copper pots of various sizes added sparkle and color from a wrought-iron pot rack hanging above the island. Cabinets in rich mahogany lined the space.

Barly handed her a goblet of Pinot Noir, and then set to work: put a pot of water on to boil for the pasta, in another pot he stirred meatballs into a thick rich tomato sauce, and turned the oven on low to warm a loaf of French bread—sliced and slathered with garlic butter.

While Barly busied himself with dinner, Maria wandered through an archway into the living room, also a statement—a man lived here. A soft brown leather couch was flanked on either side with deep, caramel-colored leather loungers.

Back in the kitchen, she saw a dining room through a swinging door, but here in the kitchen a picture window created a bright sunny breakfast nook.

"We'll eat at the counter. The mats and silverware are on the other side of the island—just nose around, and thank you."

"Thank you?"

"For accepting my invitation."

With another stir of the sauce, he dipped a wooden spoon for a taste test. I think a little more oregano. What do you think?"

Holding the spoon to her lips, Maria sampled the sauce. "Umm. I think it's perfect. When did you do all this—meatballs, sauce. I can smell the garlic on the bread."

"I confess. I hoped you would join me for dinner tonight. I just didn't anticipate it would be a therapy session—for both of us by the way. Tommy must be scared ... sorry no shoptalk until after dinner. Everything is set for a few minutes. Let me show you the addition you asked about. First, a little more vino. We'll ration ourselves tonight. I have a surgery first thing in the morning and I know you're on duty. Then there are the Caldwells. Sorry, did it again."

Waving his hand for her to follow, they walked through the living room to a paneled door. Barly turned the knob, nodding to Maria to step in. To her surprise the door opened to a large room—no walls, letting the light from the windows and three skylights fill the space. In the corner was a compact galley kitchen—sink, stovetop, countertop refrigerator with a coffeemaker next to it.

There was no furniture except for two seven-foot workbenches in the center and another workbench at the end forming a T configuration. Four wood stools were pushed randomly under the benches. Every inch of wall space was covered by shelving interspersed with large five-foot corkboards filled with pictures, all lining up over pine cabinets.

Tools were scattered on the tables: drills and drill bits, routers, sanding wheel, clamps and vices, a soup can of lead pencils along with a small hand vacuum, and brushes from fat to delicate. Barrels for woodchips were placed underneath the thick wooden planks topping the benches.

Florescent tubes between the skylights lit up the space like an operating room. Books filled most of the shelves, bits of paper sticking out of the bindings marking something of interest.

There were four carvings in different stages of creation sitting on the workbenches. Barly explained what he was hoping to achieve from one of the carvings—a deer. "I was inspired by a story my mother told me of an encounter with a fawn when she was a little girl growing up with her family, members of the Algonquin Indian tribe up north. The tribe she was born into. She's an avid painter ... well, you saw her work when you were up at the cottage, New Year's ...

"Yes, I saw them. The colors were breathtaking." Maria's heart ticked up a beat at his speaking of New Year's Eve three years ago, when—

"She met my dad at a showing of her work in Portland."

"Barly, the deer, the picture tacked on the wall ...

"Yeah, it helps with the proportions, how he's standing, the eyes alert looking at my mom."

Maria saw a figure of an old woman that he was carving, her hands gnarled from laboring in the fields.

A hissing of water splattering on the burner broke into the reveal of the man. "Oops, better get back to our dinner before something burns."

———

HITCHING UP ON THE high stool at the counter, Maria kicked off her shoes as Barly set in front of her a basket of warm French bread wrapped in a white napkin and a bowl of pasta with sauce topped with two large meatballs. Joining her with a bowl of the pasta mixture, he topped off their wine and then passed a dish with freshly grated Parmesan cheese to her.

"What time do you expect the Caldwells tomorrow?" Barly spooned fresh cheese on top of a meatball, cut it in half and popped it into his mouth.

"Around noon. I hope you'll be able to meet them."

"Wild horses couldn't keep me from being with you."

"I'll take them to the conference room off the lobby. That would be private. I'm worried that the meeting could be intimidating for them. Hospital Security, Chief Roth, Liz, Manny, you and I—"

"How should we tell them about Tabby?"

"Of course, we have to tell them—like we tell our patients bad news—outright, short, the truth."

"Telling them about Tabby, and then seeing Tommy ... it's going to be overwhelming for them. Be prepared," he said.

"Just in case you get held up, I won't say anything until you're with me."

"Maria, I'll be with you. I promise."

———

DRIVING BACK TO HER car at the hospital, they sat in a comfortable silence, each in their own thoughts, Barly's hand covering hers across the console. "Not much of a dinner date was it? We never changed out of our scrubs. Next time I'll take you to a fancy place."

"It was a wonderful evening. Your sculptures, well, you certainly inherited your mother's artistic genes."

Parking in the lot, he strolled around the car and opened her door. Turning her head resting against the headrest, she looked at him, her eyes strained, showing fatigue.

He pushed in beside her. "It's been a hard day and tomorrow won't be easy." Tilting her chin up, he scanned her violet eyes. The moment was electric and he was not about to let it go by. He slowly lowered his lips to hers. She didn't pull away, on the contrary she pressed her lips to his. His fingers threaded through her hair, then he pressed her head under his chin. "I'll follow you home. Flick the porch light when you're safe inside and I'll be on my way. Okay?"

"Okay, and thank you for a wonderful dinner ... evening."

Chapter 21

———

THERE IT WAS. The page. A Mr. and Mrs. Steven Caldwell, escorted by a neighbor, had arrived. They were waiting in the hospital's lobby.

Maria took in a sharp breath, absently touched her heart, and tapped Barly's number. "They're here. I'll meet you at the first floor elevator."

As she exited the elevator Barly touched her arm in support, a scant smile on his lips. Together they walked to the lobby to face the Caldwells.

Maria was instantly alarmed at how frail the couple looked sitting on a settee, leaning against each other, feet flat on the floor. The neighbor sat on a straight chair to their side.

"Mr. and Mrs. Caldwell, I'm Dr. Maria Grayson and this is Dr. Joe Bartholomew." Maria bent her head, grasping the woman's trembling fingers. Barly nodded to Mr. Caldwell who timidly offered his hand, shaking the doctors in greeting.

The neighbor leaned forward. "I'm Gladys. I live next door to the Caldwells. They couldn't make the trip alone. I offered to travel with them."

"Nice to meet you, Gladys," Maria said smiling at the woman, acknowledging her kindness.

"We understand you've had a trying few days to say the least." Barly's gaze moved from Mr. Caldwell to Gladys. "Have you been to see the coroner?"

Mrs. Caldwell's head dropped as her husband patted her hand. Looking up at Barly, he and Gladys nodded that they had. The couple said nothing about that stop, but the fatigue in their slumping bodies displayed their anguish.

"Let's go in the conference room," Maria said helping Mrs. Caldwell to her feet tucking the woman's arm through hers. "We'll have more privacy. How about a cup of tea, or whatever you'd like?"

Mrs. Caldwell nodded, looked to her husband as Barly's firm grip under the man's elbow helped him to stand. Once on their feet the Caldwells straightened up, gaining strength and Mr. Caldwell took over the duty of holding his wife's arm, Barly walking beside him as they followed Maria. Gladys remained a few paces behind.

Settling onto the cloth-padded chairs around the conference table, Maria sat beside Mrs. Caldwell as Barly served the tea.

With a rap on the door, Chief Roth, Officer Tracy, and Liz and Manny entered in a line introducing themselves to the Caldwells and Gladys. Roth glanced at Maria, raised his brows. Maria replied with a slight shake of her head. She had not told the Caldwells that Tabby was missing.

Maria turned to Mrs. Caldwell, gently touching the woman's fingers wrapped around the cup of tea. "We have some information for you ... about Tommy and Tabatha."

Mrs. Caldwell turned her red swollen eyes to Maria.

Barly, sitting beside Mr. Caldwell, nodded to Maria. Taking a breath, Maria plunged on. More times than she wanted to acknowledge she had sat before a patient, a patient's family, conveying bad news. She knew it was best not to beat around the bush increasing the anxiety for what was coming.

"A few days ago, early in the morning, sometime around two o'clock, your granddaughter, Tabatha, was abducted from the hospital."

Mrs. Caldwell's hand jerked from Maria's fingers, tipping over her teacup, her eyes wide in fear. Maria reached for a napkin mopping up what few drops hit the table.

Mr. Caldwell, his body shaking, rose to his feet. "For God's sake, do you know where she is?"

Barly rose but didn't touch the grandfather. At this moment Mr. Caldwell wanted answers not a restraining hand on his arm.

Maria looked at Roth for help, the latest word.

"We don't know, Mr. Caldwell, but we have a few clues. One thing I can promise you, I will give it to you straight, whatever we find." Roth's voice was steady, strong, no nonsense.

His legs buckling, Mr. Caldwell slumped down on the chair. "What clues?" His hand fumbled for his wife's, their fingers intertwining.

"We have a woman captured on the security camera leaving the hospital in the time frame the baby went missing. A very pregnant woman. We believe Tabatha was hidden beneath the woman's clothing. Seconds later, another camera captured an image of a woman getting into a car and driving out of the parking lot. It was the same woman. We have a picture that Dr. Bartholomew took of the boy with his cell the morning of the fire. Dr. Grayson took a picture of Tabatha the same morning. At that time we didn't know the infant's last name."

Caldwell's eyes scanned Roth's face. "Who took the picture of our son? Looked like he was in an operating room."

"I took that picture." Barly was sitting next to Mr. Caldwell, his eyes full of sympathy for the gentleman. "I tried to save your son. He never gained consciousness since the time the medics transported him to the hospital from the church. His heart gave out, sir."

"Never had a heart problem before." The elder's retort was sharp, eyes squinting at Barly, his conclusion was obvious. *This man killed my son.*

"I tried. He did not suffer, Mr. Caldwell. I'm sorry."

Mr. Caldwell said nothing more, only stared at the doctor sitting next to him.

Roth cut into the silence. "We've issued an APB, all points bulletin with the image of the woman on the camera to our field agents in the New England states, and to the main office in all the states around the country." Roth did not divulge that the second camera did not get a full license plate number, or that the car had not been found, or that they had no clue as to who the woman was.

Barly glanced at Maria, then back to Mr. Caldwell. "Mr. Caldwell, your son died saving his children. He—"

"The boy is not my son's child. He's the tramp's son. She had him, a year old when she met Stevie. She trapped Stevie. Let him get her pregnant. Our son was a good man. He married her. Was going to adopt the boy." His words came in spurts, sucking in air between each utterance.

"Do you know where your son's wife is?" Manny asked leaning forward, centering the lined-yellow pad of paper in front of him, fingers holding his pen, poised, hoping to hear something of value.

Mrs. Caldwell spoke for the first time. Her voice low, raspy. "Stevie was a Sergeant in the Army. After he was wounded in Afghanistan he spent months at Walter Reed where, after numerous operations, he was fitted with a mechanical leg. He found an apartment, a room really, in Raleigh. He wanted to be near us but enough of a drive that, I suppose, he felt we wouldn't interfere with his rehabilitation. He met Trixie ... she was a singer in a bar. Trixie, that's her stage name, and the name she goes by. Her real name is Trisandra, anyway, Trixie left our Stevie right after Tabatha was born. Stevie told us she ran off with a bandleader from Canada, a man who promised her a big singing career. The fire happened on a Sunday. He probably stopped at the church asking for help from the good Lord. He was on his way to Quebec ... somewhere in Canada, to find her. That's why he was in Maine, on his way ..." Mrs. Caldwell wiped a tear from her cheek, unable to continue speaking.

Liz helped herself to the carafe of tea and a cup for Manny. Returning to the table, she asked the Caldwells' if they knew Trixie's parents.

Mr. Caldwell patted his wife's hand. He would answer the question. "Never asked about her family, don't even know her last name. Our son did the honorable thing and married her, said he loved her, but she was the reason we became estranged from him. We saw Stevie and her son twice. Once when he told us they were getting married and then a few months before she gave birth to the baby. Stevie wanted to patch things up with us. But it didn't work out. We wanted nothing to do with the tramp. But when Trixie took off, he was so distraught that he stopped by to see us, told us where he was going and that he was taking Tommy and Tabatha with him. I guess that makes it three times that we saw Tommy."

"What about Tommy?" Manny asked glancing at Barly, back to Mr. Caldwell.

"Yes, Stevie said the boy was with him."

"Would you like to see, Tommy? We can go up—" Maria stopped.

Mr. Caldwell's eyes closed to a squint, his jaw muscles tightened, lips clamped shut. He looked at his wife.

Mrs. Caldwell patted her husband's hand, answered for both of them. "Yes, for Stevie."

———

THE GROUP WALKED IN silence to the elevator, riding to the second floor. The Caldwells again followed Maria, Gladys bringing up the rear.

Entering the ward, they saw Tommy clutching his teddy bear.

Maria and Barly held back, as step by painful step the grandparents approached the boy. A tear dropped to Mrs. Caldwell's cheek as her husband bent down to the crib. Tommy timidly circled his little arms around the old man's neck.

"You be a good boy for these doctors, Tommy. They will take care of you." Pulling the chubby little arms away from his neck, Mr. Caldwell turned, grasped his wife's arm and marched her out of the ward to the elevator.

Barly grabbed Maria's arm as she whirled to the Caldwells.

Breathing hard, fists jammed to her side, she looked like she could kill them both for their treatment of Tommy. Jerking away from Barly, she marched after them. The rest of the group followed in her wake.

"Wait just a minute," Maria said as she halted in front of Mr. and Mrs. Caldwell. "You can't abandon Tommy. When are you going to take custody of Tabatha *and* Tommy?" Hands balled at her side, Maria's violet eyes turned black.

The Caldwells stared at the women in front of them, turned as the elevator door pulled back, and stepped in. Mr. Caldwell's finger hovering over the first floor elevator button.

Eyes darting from one to the other, the group entered the elevator, riding down in silence. Exiting the elevator, the Caldwells turned to face Maria and Barly.

Mrs. Caldwell looked to her husband then to Maria. "My husband isn't well. We couldn't possibly care for Tabatha. And Steven would never want Tommy in our house."

"Take Tommy? Never," Mr. Caldwell said angrily. "As far as we're concerned, the tramp stole our son away from us. We *would* like to know when you find the baby, but we could never be able to care for her."

Gaining strength from their anger, the couple quickly marched out of the hospital. Gladys shook her head, sighing. "I'm sorry," she said softly, then rushed to catch up with her neighbors.

The group stood rooted to the floor watching the Caldwells as they left. There was nothing more to say. Roth returned to the station, Tracy to the hospital security office, and Liz and Manny excused themselves, mumbling to Maria that they would see her later.

Maria nodded to each as they left but continued to stare out the glass doors, as Gladys drove the Caldwells out of the parking lot.

"Come on, Dr. Grayson, let's grab what's left of the tea before rounds." Barly put his hand on her shoulder guiding her away from the image of the retreating grandparents.

In the conference room, Barly divided the last of the tea into cups. Taking a seat facing each other across a corner of the table, Maria looked down, shoulders drooping, still trying to process the last hour and the lack of compassion they showed little Tommy.

"So, Dr. Grayson, what's your take on the grandparents—what they thought about their son's wife and their lack of concern for Tommy?"

"I don't know what to make of them. They made me so mad. The disrespect for the kid's mother. What did *you* think about Mr. Caldwell's reaction to Tommy? I wanted to smack him the way he yanked Tommy's little arms away."

Barly thought a minute, sipped his tea. "They were honest, overwhelmed. I can relate. At their age the thought of a little person, or two, under their care, how children would interrupt their routine ..."

Maria glanced over the rim of her teacup. What did he just say? Maybe she had misjudged this man, misjudged him as a dad ... he was kind, a brilliant doctor, but he did like his toys. Children would disrupt, no, the word he used was interrupt ... children would interrupt his routine.

Barly looked away, across the room. "You're becoming too attached, Maria. You know you have to be careful of the doctor-patient relationship. Like it or not, the Caldwells are the next of kin unless the mother shows up."

Maria's teacup hit the saucer as she shot up off the chair. "I *am* being careful, careful enough to consider that if the Caldwells don't want Tabatha and Tommy, then by God maybe I can find a way to make sure they have a loving home."

Barly, startled by the anger of her words, which were obviously directed at him, watched as the conference room door slammed behind her.

Chapter 22

———

THE TEENAGE LOVERS BELIEVED sex was so much more exhilarating after inhaling a freshly rolled marijuana joint. Even though the baby had finally cried itself to sleep, they were having second thoughts. Maybe it wasn't such a good idea to have a baby. Cindy flopped her head back against the seat, her druggy eyes gazing through the windshield of the beat-up green Chevy as the early morning sunrise crested the ocean's horizon. Drawing a final puff, she opened the car door, flicking the stubby butt out onto the cracked cement parking lot.

"Ike, I need more. My skin is crawling. Come on, Ike, you promised."

Ike grabbed two syringes filled with the purest stuff he ever bought. He had prepared the snow squatting on the ground behind a dumpster, Cindy knelt next to him, anticipation in her eyes. He smiled at Cindy taking hold of her arm, carefully inserting the needle. With a slight wince she closed her eyes waiting to feel heat flow in her belly.

"Hurry, Cindy, shoot me."

Cindy kept her eyes shut.

"Come on, C. Here, shoot."

Cindy frowned but did as she was told.

"Okay, baby, let's go down to the water. It'll be great, the waves hitting our skin as we soar."

Closing the car door, her eyes lolled over to her eighteen-year-old lover.

Grasping each other's hand, they stumbled over the sand to the gentle waves, and then waded into the cool ocean water. Impatient to feel her breasts, Ike's hands crawled up underneath Cindy's red T-shirt, then he stripped her jeans, his jeans, and together their bodies rode the waves.

"Someone's opening your car door," she murmured, her head resting on his shoulder.

"So what. Maybe they'll take the screamer. I much prefer you, Cindy baby, you feel so good."

"So do you, Ike. These waves ... the waves ... oh, Ike, ... I love you."

———

"WHAT THE HELL? A BABY?" Kim looked around. Where were the parents? Scanning the beach, then the water, she saw two heads bobbing together. "Hey, your baby's crying. Stupid kids," she murmured. "Little one ... come here, there, there, shhh." Kim lifted the baby, cradling it in her arms. With the smell of poop, she put the infant back in the car seat, grabbed the diaper bag and carried the crying baby in the infant seat to her car.

Sliding into the back seat, she shoved the clothes, pillow and blanket to the floor. "Sorry, kid, there's not much room to change you. You see I'm living in this hunk of metal on account of I was fired from my job."

The baby let out a scream.

"There, there. I cried just like you—for days, weeks even. They said I wasn't a responsible person. Always late. Well, they were late, too. Hypocrites."

Rooting around the diaper bag, she found a bottle of water with an inverted nipple. Screwing the nipple so the baby could suck, the crying eased, then stopped, replaced with a hungry sucking sound.

"So, kid, I couldn't pay my rent. That's what happens when you grow up—you have to pay rent, or you live in your car."

Kim's free hand searched the bag for something to clean the baby's bottom with and pulled out a new disposable diaper with an envelope stuck to it. No, not an envelope, an airline folder. "Would you look at that? A ticket to San Francisco for one, and dollar bills, no three one-hundred dollar bills, and ... five twenties."

Kim glanced out at the water. She couldn't see the bobbing heads in the bright rays of the sun, and no one was on the beach. Looking under the ticket she found a printed email. As she read the message her eyes popped wide. "Oh, my God, this baby is stolen. And here ... delivery instructions? $10,000??? OH MY GOD! Baby girl, you are my angel!"

Securing the infant seat, and then climbing into the front behind the wheel, Kim started the car, backed out of the parking space, and drove out of sight down the road turning at the arrow pointing to the airport.

Looking in the rearview mirror at the blue-eyed angel, tears of joy welled in Kim's eyes.

"Wait. Wait. Wait. I have to call ... what did the email say? Oh, yes, I'm supposed to say that I have your package. Baby girl, we have to do this like they said." Kim continued to rattle on to the baby in the mirror. "Get a grip, Kim girl. This is big crime stuff. If you don't do this right, instead of being homeless you'll be in a jail cell. Think. You can't use your phone. You need change for a payphone, like from one of those twenties." Giggles erupted from her lips.

Spotting a 7-Eleven on the corner, Kim slowed, engaged her turn signal and pulled into a parking space. One thing was for sure, she was not going to be picked up for speeding, and she wasn't going to let anyone else have her baby. Cradling the infant, kissing her downy blonde hair, Kim entered the convenience store.

She picked out a candy bar and a small carton of milk. Surely the baby would be happier with something more substantial than water in her tummy. Heading to the checkout counter she spotted a display: *Disposable phone $10.* How perfect was that? Call the number in the email from the privacy of her car.

Paying for her purchases, Kim hustled out of the store, unlocked the car door, and slid into the back seat. She smiled, with any luck she would be sleeping on an airplane and not in her car tonight. Wow, with 10K she'd be able to stay in a motel, maybe get an apartment.

Fixing the baby's bottle, then holding the bottle to the baby's mouth, Kim tapped in the phone number from the email.

"Hello," a woman answered.

"Mrs. Sinclair, please."

"Whose calling?"

"Ah, ah, a friend of Cookie's."

Kim heard a finger snapping. Excited whispering.

"How is Cookie? Is she there?"

"She's fine and, no, she isn't here. Haven't seen her ... never mind about Cookie. I have your email, Mrs. Sinclair, and I'm holding the ticket and the money you sent with the ticket. I also have the package you mention in your email. I presume you would still pay for delivery?"

More whispering. Kim couldn't make out what they were saying.

"Yes, we will pay for delivery. Where are you and how do you happen to have the ... the package?"

"I'm near the Boston airport and how I happen to have the baby, the package, doesn't matter a fig leaf. What matters is that I need a valid ticket along with expense money. The ticket is to be in my name so I can get through security. And while you're at it include a ticket for the baby so I won't have to hold her. My name: Kim Trotter."

"All right, Ms. Trotter. My husband will make the arrangements, same airline. It's early so I think he should be able to arrange for you to take the next flight ... wait just a minute."

More whispering.

"The flight will leave in two hours, which, if you are near the airport as you say, should give you time. I'll email you with more instructions. What is your email address?"

"Sorry, Mrs. Sinclair, but I don't have a computer and even if I did I wouldn't give you my email address. I won't recognize you, but you can recognize me. I'll be carrying a baby, probably screaming baby, and I'm wearing a Boston Celtic T-shirt. That should do it. I'm leaving now and I'll be at the ticket counter in about thirty minutes. I'm sure there'll be a Western Union located nearby. When you wire the money make it the closest one to the airline ticket counter. If I have a problem, I'll call you again. I presume you will stay close to your phone. And one more thing. The price for delivery is now double. After all, it has been very trying for me. Do we have a deal or do I call the police?"

Whispering!

"Of course, you have a deal. Now, please be careful. If we don't hear from you my husband and I will be under the assumption that all the arrangements met with your satisfaction. We'll be in the baggage area at San Francisco International Airport. Just in case you wonder about the couple walking up to you, I'll be wearing a dark purple jumpsuit. My husband will be wearing a light tan summer suit. Have a good flight, my dear. And, *please* take care of the package. A damaged delivery will result in no delivery payment. Do I make myself clear?"

"Perfectly!"

Chapter 23

———

THE DAY DIDN'T END with the Caldwells, or the harsh words she threw at Barly, emergencies sprang up until Maria thought she was treating every child in York—a broken arm, an asthma attack, fevers. Parents were frantic, fearing the worst, faces pleading for Dr. Grayson to help save their child.

It was almost ten o'clock when Maria returned home to join her friends around the kitchen table. Liz and Manny were laughing so hard their eyes were tearing from Stella relating how she wangled a dinner invitation from Waldo. Seems the Vet was checking Jenny's paw when the dog slurped his cheek. Stella suggested instead of a slurp she'd like to repay him with dinner. He shyly, so adorably, according to Stella, suggested they go to his house which was attached to his clinic. That way Jenny could join them and Stella wouldn't have to take her home first, or worse, put the poor thing in a wire cage. After all, the dog whimpered whenever the Vet touched her paw.

While Waldo was closing the clinic, Stella leaned down, patted Jenny, saying that she was a real ham, a true doggie friend, thanking Jenny for her unwavering support. Whispering in Jenny's silky ear, Stella added that if she kept up the doggie-act, there was a monster bone in her future. Waldo finished locking up, checked one last time on his patients, and then led Stella and Jenny through a short hallway, through a door, into his very cozy home.

The tale finished, Stella laughed again, reaching down to caress her friend.

The merriment stopped abruptly when Maria stepped into the kitchen.

Stella needed only one look at her housemate to know the doctor's day had not gone well. "You're beat. Sit. Manny, pour the weary girl a glass of wine while I warm up her dinner." Stella retrieved a foam container from the refrigerator, food she had picked up for Maria after she left Waldo.

Liz gave Maria a hug and with raised brows—don't mess with me—nudged her into a chair. "Stella, I think we're going to need another bottle of wine. Tell me where and I'll get it."

"In that pantry-like cupboard, other side of the fridge, Liz. Get two bottles while you're at it, Manny just killed the last one." Transferring the entrée from the white foam box to a microwavable plate, a quick zap, and with a triumphant look, Stella placed the dish in front of Maria.

Spaghetti!

Wincing, Maria closed her eyes, drew a breath, and flashed a weak smile of thanks to Stella.

"What's the matter? You suddenly have an aversion to pasta?" Stella hot footed it to the counter, zapped a baguette slathered with garlic butter. With a slab of cheese, a couple of knives, forks, and plates, she had served up a party.

No one seemed ready to party, but they were hungry.

"Maria, Liz told me about the Caldwells. How heartless can they be to a little boy?" Serving the warm bread in a dinner-napkin blanket, Stella took a sip of wine as she plopped on a chair.

"Oh, Stel, that's not fair. They had just seen their son in the morgue an hour earlier. I'm afraid I was the callous one. Manny, any leads on Tabby?"

"No, but Liz and I have an idea. Actually, Chief Roth already gave us the go ahead—for the idea, but no manpower."

"What's the idea?" Maria poked at the pasta with her fork, then took a bite of warm, crusty garlic bread, her eyes roving from Manny to Liz.

"A tip line. The chief's conference room has a perfect setup. Stella said she could help man the phones—only two phones but—"

"How do you plan to get the story out?" Maria was suddenly hungry. Her PI's were on the hunt, and had come up with a plan of action.

"Easy peasy, girlfriend." Liz and Stella exchanged smirks. "We give the media a news update on the Miracle Baby rescued from a church fire a few days ago. Sadly, she's been kidnapped and the authorities are seeking your help," Liz said mimicking a somber female TV reporter.

Three sets of eyes over three grinning lips waited for Maria's reaction.

"A news update is a great idea, and, Stel, here's another thought I had today. What would you say if I brought Tommy here … to stay with us until … well until …

"For as long as you want, Maria. Let's see, I'll call Harriett. She dog sat for you … you know … back then. Loves Jenny, and vice versa. "

"That was years ago, Stel."

"I know, but I hear she just retired, so I bet we could lure her away from those TV sitcoms with Jenny."

Hearing her name, Jenny issued a half bark trotting with a bit of a limp to Maria, nudging her arm with her nose. "Okay, give Harriett a try."

"What about Barly being part of the news update? The picture of him holding Tommy as he carried him out of the church was enough to break your heart." Liz said as Manny leaned in with a peck on his wife's cheek.

"I don't think so." Maria gazed into her wine glass. "He has a heavy schedule with his practice. He wouldn't have time. No way would he *interrupt* his routine."

The three grins turned upside down. Now what was wrong? What was rankling Maria?

Chapter 24

———

MISERABLE, DRAWN TO MAKE amends, Maria sat in her car in Barly's driveway staring at the closed garage door. She knew he was furious with her after their angry exchange yesterday when the Caldwells left. She had stalked off to her car and caught him leaving the conference room stalking off in the other direction to his car.

Well, like it or not, they were both wrapped up with the two children who had a grip on their heartstrings, and, no matter what Barly said, Maria knew he cared. She was still furious at the Caldwells, so unfeeling. How could Mr. Caldwell have pulled away from Tommy leaving him crying.

If their mother didn't show up soon, or if the grandparents didn't change their minds, then Children's Services would come for Tommy. *If* … no, *when* Tabby was found, Maria could only stall a few days under the pretense of examining the baby before releasing her. Adoption? If only she could. She decided to talk to Manny and Liz, get their thoughts on whether she had a chance to adopt them, even if there was no *we*.

Barly hadn't come to the front door, so he must be in his workshop. The shop's front door was painted black which was likely going to be his mood. It was ajar so she surmised he was working on one of his sculptures.

With a sigh, she slid out from behind the steering wheel, walked across a patch of grass to the black door, removing her camera from her bag. The birds were singing, the sun was shining, and a soft breeze rustled through the leaves of a large oak tree. How little Tommy would love it here, but it wasn't Barly's house, it was her house she was proposing to bring him to … temporarily.

Approaching the black door, she snapped a picture of a squirrel holding an acorn on the doorstep just as the door jerked open wide. Barly filled the camera lens, hands on his hips, eyes in a dark stare stopping her in her tracks.

Her hands fell to her side. Her voice soft, she spoke rapidly. "I'm sorry. I shouldn't have left the hospital so quickly. Can we talk?" Could he see her heart beating wildly under her white silk shirt? What if he told her to get lost?

Barly turned away from the door leaving it open.

He must mean for her to follow ... didn't he? She stepped inside. He was standing at the picture window, hands laced behind his neck. In all likelihood he had seen her drive in but couldn't bring himself to greet her.

Setting her shoulder bag on the hardwood floor, she pulled out an extra stool from under his workbench. Not long ago she had sat in this very spot listening to his passionate description of his wood carvings.

Ignoring his back, she began to relate what she hoped would be plans they could come together on for Tommy. "I talked to Stella, told her how awful the Caldwells acted. I still can't get the image out of my mind of Mr. Caldwell pulling little Tommy's pudgy arms away."

"So, you talked to Stella. That's nice. What did the two of you cook up?"

"Barly, I said I was sorry. I shouldn't have—"

"When you're cornered you retreat inside yourself. You asked for my opinion, didn't like it, and marched off. Yes, I thought the Caldwells' actions were abhorrent, unforgivable." He whirled away from the window, took a step to the bench staring down at her, fingers gripping the edge. "Your walls went up so fast they almost knocked me over."

Maria's head jerked back at the blow. Had she really unconsciously put up such a barrier? A place she had built to hide herself over the years. The only one she could depend on was herself. She had hoped Mac would be the one to pull her from her demons, but they were so different. She realized quickly that she loved him, but not so quick to realize that she loved him only as the patient she had grown to care for when he was first brought into her ER, bloody, clinging to life.

Oh, God, what had she done? The man standing before her made her heart race, made her blood rush hot down and through her stomach. She knew it the minute he kissed her over two years ago at his cottage on Moosehead Lake on New Year's Eve. She fought hard then against the urgent desire for him, the feelings of never wanting to be away from him. But by morning she had regained her composure, and, as he said, retreated behind walls.

"Barly, please, don't look at me that way. Do you believe in fate?"

"I believe in science. Humans have a way of stabbing fate in the belly."

"The fire, Tabby and Tommy, you and I. If we hadn't gone into that church to look for the children that woman warned us were trapped, they would have died along with their father. Barly, we're their guardians, like it or not. I want to bring Tommy to my house. I'm asking you to be a father figure to him. He needs you. I'm praying that Tabby is found soon so they can be together again."

"And just how is that supposed to work? Joint custody but you establishing yourself as the main caretaker ... your house? Gee whiz, how kind of you." He turned back to the window but his voice had softened.

"It's only a temporary solution. We have to get him out of the sterile hospital environment. Everyone loves him, but it's not home. My schedule will be difficult for another six months until I complete my residency and can find a permanent position. And your schedule, well you're on call night and day, weekends, but together I think we can work something out with the help of a nanny."

"My child raised by a nanny?"

There it was. He not only had strong feelings for the toddler but had taken him to his heart as his own.

"I thought if we hired someone to help ... someone we both respect."

He turned back to her, arms crossed, but the anger had gone. His shoulders relaxed. He pushed his high carving stool under him, rested one foot on a rung, hands on his thighs, eyes returning to their warm gray.

Maria saw him soften, begin to cotton to the thought of her plan.

"Harriett, Dr. Farnsworth's former office manager, just retired. She'd be perfect. Can you picture it, how Tommy is going to love Jenny? She'll protect him, play with him. Harriett can take them to her house during our work hours if she wants. They can come here when you're home, my house when I'm home."

"Your house? My house? Harriett's house? Wow, that's stable. You have to be kidding."

"Well, when you put it like that—" Maria's head drooped. He was right. She was wrong. He wasn't enamored with her idea. What was she thinking?

Barly's fingers fidgeted with a chisel. "You're making a lot of assumptions. Will the hospital release them to our care? Hell, Child Services would never agree?" He saw her wall crumble leaving her vulnerable, wounded, and he had stupidly gone in for the kill. How could he have done that? He looked over at her, her fingers fondling some wood chips. But he knew she was strong, and would gather herself together, putting up yet another barricade. He couldn't let that happen. She didn't know it, but she was crying out for his help. He reached across the bench, laid his hand over hers. Her fingers tightened on the chips but did not pull away.

"Maria, the Caldwells' reaction to Tommy and the abduction of Tabby were body blows to both of us. We can't solve everything at once. Your idea of getting Tommy out of the hospital is a good first step. I think we can get permission, as his doctors, to gain temporary care of him … not guardians, way too early and complicated for that. If you want to bring him home with you, then I'll go along. And, go ahead and talk to Harriett. We have to have someone lined up before we approach the hospital administration about bringing him home … *temporarily*."

"Home. Sounds nice, don't you think?" Her eyes, full of hope, raised to his.

The warmth in her voice melted his heart. "Yes, sounds nice. How about we go to the hospital to see Tommy? Poor tyke was crying crocodile tears the last time I left him. He'll think we've abandoned him. Then, with any luck, we can sneak out, without being pulled into an emergency surgery, and have a drink at the

Antlers. A noisy bar will be just the ticket to cope with those nasty Caldwells, don't you think?" Barly tried to smile. He wasn't sure he pulled it off, bringing her back to him without the walls.

"Sounds about right ... a noisy bar. I have more to tell you ... Liz and Manny's idea for a press conference ... a tip line requiring *manpower.*"

Chapter 25

———

San Francisco, California

THE PATIO PHONE RANG a third time. Diane Thompson called out to Mai Linh, her housekeeper for fifteen years, to *please* answer the phone now sounding-off for the fourth time. Pulling off her gardening gloves, Diane rushed to answer ring five, grabbing the cordless receiver from the cradle.

"Oh, Mrs. Thompson, I'm so happy to hear your voice. I thought for a minute you were going to miss my call and I'd have to contact the next couple on my list."

"Sorry, Mrs. Sinclair. I'm tending my roses and Mai Linh seems to be out of earshot. What's up?"

"Oh, my dear, the most wonderful news. I believe we have the perfect baby for you. She was supposed to be adopted by another couple but they walked away at the last minute, something about not being able to afford the adoption at this time. So this sweet infant is available. Your life will be full again since the tragic loss of your husband."

"Really? How old is she? Healthy? When can I see her?" Diane fumbled to remove her wide-brim straw hat. *A baby! Oh, please dear God let her be mine.* Running up the stairs struggling to remove her blouse, racing to the bathroom, turning on the shower, holding the phone, listening to catch every word that Susan Sinclair said.

"She's adorable, Mrs. Thompson. She's a healthy two-month-old little girl. Blue eyes just like yours. Actually, if you can come down to the orphanage right now you can take her home with you."

"Now? I can have her now?"

"The adoption papers will be ready in two days. They are being signed, processed, and we should receive them in the overnight mail. Of course, we have to make sure everything is in order before we finalize the adoption in two days, as I said. If you come now with your payment, she's yours. Otherwise, well, we will have to contact the next couple on our list."

"No, no. I'm coming. *Please*, don't call anyone else. I'm coming. I'm coming."

"Well, they are very anxious, and offered another $10,000 if they could have the next available infant. But you've been waiting a long time and Jeffrey and I think she is perfect for you. What do you say? Can you be here by noon?"

"Yes, before noon. Yes, of course, I can. I'll have the cashier's check you requested. $190,000?"

"That's right, Mrs. Thompson. Check the list I gave you. Make sure you have everything—infant seat is critical so she'll be safe in the car when you drive her *home*."

"Yes, yes, *home*. I have everything packed. Oh, thank you, Mrs. Sinclair."

Diane disconnected the call and raced from the shower to her closet, pushing hangers one after the other to the side, deciding on a blue crepe dress, laying it on the bed. She raced to the hall, called over the second-floor railing to her housekeeper. "Mai Linh, come here, come here. I have a baby ... a *baby!*"

Hustling to the stairs, Mai Linh looked up, "Mrs. Thompson, I'm sorry—in the basement. I didn't hear the phone. So sorry." At fifty-nine, the Vietnamese widow wasn't as quick as she used to be. "The orphanage called?"

"Yes, isn't it wonderful? You must come with me. I need your help. The nursery..."

Mai Linh ran up the curving stairs following Diane into the nursery.

"It looks in order ... do you see anything else she'll need?" Diane asked caressing the bassinet dotted with silk rosebuds.

"Mrs. Thompson, a baby girl?" Mai Linh stood grinning at her. "Everything is beautiful. You finish dressing. I'll change and meet you in the garage. Here, give me that infant seat."

"Oh, thank you, dear. I'd be lost without you. A baby, Mai Linh, a baby girl."

Chapter 26

———

IT WAS A MIRACLE. Diane pinched herself to be sure she wasn't dreaming. Rocking her adorable new baby, she marveled at her tiny fingers, her big blue eyes, at each little move she made. At the moment she was sucking hungrily on the bottle of formula. Every other suck the baby screamed and then attacked the nipple again.

The moment Diane got home she had carried her baby to the nursery to change her. Maybe a wet diaper was causing her to cry. The new mother was startled at the infant's raw bottom. Whoever had been caring for her must not have changed her regularly. But Mrs. Sinclair said their doctor had given her a thorough checkup and that she was a healthy baby. Her skin was soft, pink … a nice plump baby. But she seemed very agitated. Suddenly, Diane thought maybe the birth mother was on drugs or an alcoholic. That could account for the baby's distress. When the infant cried her little body quivered no matter how Diane tried to comfort her.

Mai Linh poked her head in the door. "Everything all right, Mrs. Thompson? I heard the cry—"

"Everything is fine Mai Linh. A diaper rash and I think she's scared, after all she's been through so much—leaving one mother and now a new mother, a new home. Don't you think that would explain her sudden outbursts?"

"Oh yes, poor thing. But now that baby has a fine home and a mother who will love her. The baby monitors are all working. I checked every room."

"Thank you, Mai Linh."

"Mrs. Thompson, I bet your husband is smiling down from heaven seeing you rocking that baby girl. If you need anything, I'll be in the kitchen."

Gazing at the baby, Diane smiled thinking fondly of her husband.

They had wanted a baby but it never happened and then suddenly he had a heart attack and was gone from her life. She was so lonely, withdrawing from her friends. Then her spirits lifted, her depression vanished when she saw a small article in the social pages of the Sunday paper a few months ago. The story was about a woman who was ecstatic over the adoption of a baby through a local San Francisco orphanage. It was quick and the owner, a Mrs. Sinclair, couldn't have been kinder.

Diane searched the internet and found the orphanage's extensive website. She hesitated then called Mrs. Sinclair the next day. The website related successful adoptions of orphans including the opportunity, on a rare occasion, to adopt a very young orphan, a baby even.

As the baby quivered in her arms, an uneasy feeling began creeping through Diane's veins. When she picked up the baby and gave Mrs. Sinclair the baby's name to enter on the adoption papers, the woman seemed tense. Oh, she smiled, was thoughtful, but after receiving the check she hurried Diane and baby Gwen out to her car. Nothing except the baby and the check had changed hands. Odd, with all the complicated legal requirements entailed for an adoption.

When Diane had inquired about meeting the surrogate mother, Mrs. Sinclair said she'd try, but the mother had left the state and she had not heard from her since.

Gwen fell asleep in Diane's arms. Poor baby, she was exhausted from her trying day. Diane carefully rose from the rocking chair and gently laid Gwen in the white bassinet adorned with little rosebuds and white tulle circling the small wicker bed. Diane tucked a pink receiving blanket around the little doll and kissed the top of her downy head. Gwen jerked at the touch but didn't open her eyes.

Her baby was so precious.

How could a mother give her up?

How could she be left at the orphanage one minute and in Diane's arm's the next without any evidence of a receipt for a baby?

A cashier's check.

Anyone could cash it.

This wasn't how Mrs. Sinclair had described a possible adoption. She had made a cursory visit to the house to verify that a baby would be well cared for. But at the time, she also gave every indication that once a baby was available the process could take a couple of days, at the very least, before the infant would be released. Then there would be two additional visits to ensure that the adoptive mother bonded with the baby before the adoption was final.

The unease Diane felt began to grow. Pacing in the library, her eyes kept returning to the telephone on her desk. Maybe she should call someone ... but she didn't want to risk losing Gwen. On the other hand, if she had her baby unlawfully she was at risk of losing her anyway.

A cable news report flashed through her mind. The news anchor reported how a detective had reunited an abducted infant with his parents, and, with the parent's help, broke an underground ring trafficking in children.

Then there was a news report this morning that a miracle baby saved in a church fire had gone missing. The baby's picture flashed on the screen. That was before she had picked up Gwen. All Diane could remember was that the baby was cute. Of course, Diane didn't write down the number ... a tip line. Where was that fire?

Diane ambled back to the nursery, watching Gwen sleep. The fringes of her lashes were clamped down against her soft skin, so peaceful.

Her baby.

Still ...

Tiptoeing out of the new nursery, Diane returned to the library, turned on her computer. In the Google search box, she typed in a few keywords: miracle baby, fire, tip line.

She was startled at the speed of the search results.

Diane picked up the phone. It couldn't hurt to check. Or could it result in losing Gwen? Diane set the receiver back down in the cradle, a fight churning inside her stomach. Should she call ... or, not?

Chapter 27

———

DIANE HURRIED BACK TO the nursery. She had to see her baby. Was she real? Yes, she was real—her precious baby, so adorable, lying in the bassinet, sleeping. Diane kissed Gwen's little hand then, leaving the door open a crack in case Gwen cried out for her, Diane quickly walked down the carpeted hallway to her bedroom. If she was going to act, she had to do it now before she lost her nerve.

Jamming her fist in her pocket, she pulled out the folded piece of pink stationery, the paper with the tip-line number, smoothing out the creases with her fingers. Fear coupled with moral conviction that she was doing the right thing, she jabbed at the buttons on the phone then instantly slammed the receiver down before the call was connected.

What was she doing? Her breath came in gasps, mouth open, gulping for air. She'd never been in trouble. Her husband's real estate business provided her with the best of everything. He took care of everything. She lacked for nothing except for the treasure lying in the bassinet down the hall.

Diane sat staring at the number she scribbled with shaky fingers a short time ago. The number was almost unreadable. Glancing at the clock—7:35 in the evening—perhaps it was too late in the day to call. She certainly wasn't going to leave a message for fear someone would trace her to the orphanage, to the Sinclairs.

Now, she was being foolish. "Come on, Diane. You have to find out. Everything is probably fine. Get yourself a glass of wine. Call from the kitchen phone." Yes, the sterile white kitchen, quite detached from the newly appointed nursery ... the baby.

Picking up the pink slip of paper, Diane slowly went down the stairs, concentrating on her breathing, calming her heart rate, careful not to trip on her silky blue caftan flowing behind her. Sitting at the kitchen desk Mai Linh used to order groceries, check on a flower delivery, call a list of people with lunch invitations, Diane took a sip of wine. With the scribbled number, a pad of paper and pen neatly lined up on the desk in front of her, she slowly, with deliberation, tapped each number. Holding the receiver to her ear she listened to the ring.

———

"TIP LINE, YORK, MAINE."

"I'm calling about a news report I saw on TV earlier."

"Hi. Thank you for calling. My name is Liz. Do you have information regarding the miracle baby?"

"I'm not sure ... I ... probably nothing."

"Take your time. It can be difficult to reach out ... sometimes you just have a feeling about something. You've seen something. So often it's the smallest piece of information that can help. Unfortunately many babies go missing. Can you describe the infant you're calling about ... you know, the age, race ..."

"Yes, I'm told she's two months old, white—"

"You were told? Is this infant with you now?" Liz jumped to her feet, snapping her fingers at Manny who had entered the room with the cup of caffeine buzz she had requested. Waving at him to pick up the phone, line two, mouthing, "Trace it! Trace it!"

"Yes." The lady caller was hesitant, but she went on. "I'm adopting the baby. I'm sure I'm mistaken, but I just want to check that everything is in order. Even though I've had her for only a few hours, I love her, and—"

"What agency are you working with? Maybe I can set your mind at ease?"

"An orphanage. They're very nice, helpful, protective of the children in their care. I must be mistaken. Thank you—"

"Wait, wait, you're probably right," Liz spoke softly, calmly, but her feet were skipping in all directions. She pushed the chair out of the way, her eyes wide, riveted on the phone, then up at Manny, back to the phone.

Manny nodded—tracing started. He was prepared. Chief Roth went through the department's protocol, the procedure to trace a call when the tip line was set up. There was a laptop at the end of the table with a wifi connection to the phone lines. He mouthed back to Liz, "Keep her talking. Keep talking," never taking his eyes from the computer screen: *San Francisco, Mrs. Diane Thompson.*

Liz continued engaging the caller, trying her best not to spook her. "I'm sure you'd feel more confident in the adoption of the baby that you already love by allaying any of your concerns. Babies are so adorable, and I'm sure she is too. Does she have brown eyes?"

Manny held his cell phone to his ear, talking in hushed tones to a San Francisco PD Detective, informing him why he was calling, that he had a tipster on the line from San Francisco, giving him the tipster's name, asking him to hold on, that he was waiting on a private investigator handling the tip line. She was trying to pry a critical piece of information from the caller.

"Oh, no, big blue eyes. Poor little thing was quivering, but she's sleeping now."

Manny tapped his pen nervously on the table his eyes glued on Liz.

"Blue eyes. How pretty." Liz did a fist pump in the air, bouncing from foot to foot. "You're doing a good job. Can I have your name, you know I have to log the calls or I get yelled at, Mrs. ... Mrs."

"Oh, I don't know. Is my call confidential?"

"Yes, all tips are confidential. Information only given to a person who is helping to find the baby."

"Okay. My name is Diane Thompson. My husband died two years ago. Please, I don't want to make any trouble for the orphanage. And, absolutely not a word to the press. My name, well, just let me say I'd become a news story if a reporter got wind of my call."

"Diane, I understand. One question, if you please. Does the baby have any identifying marks on her body? You know, just so we can put your mind at ease. Anything unusual?"

"Well, yes, I was going to ask Susan, my contact, at the orphanage. When I brought Gwen home, she was quivering even after her bottle and I thought a nice warm bath might help her. She had a bad diaper rash. She's a beautiful baby. Perfect except for the little toe on her left foot, the baby toe. The tip, the nail is missing."

"The toe is missing? Left foot?" Liz could hardly contain her excitement. Manny was grinning, listening to the caller in one ear and relating the information to the San Francisco detective.

"That's right. It looked to me like it had been surgically removed or cut somehow in an accident. It's healing but still looks like she lost it recently."

Manny was furiously writing on a piece of paper, sliding it in front of Liz. Detective Steele, San Francisco PD, is on his way to Diane. Keep talking. 5 min. Tell her to ask for ID.

"Diane, I don't want to scare you, please be strong, but you may be a victim of a very cruel crime. From the information you have given me, it is very possible the baby in your care is the missing miracle baby we are desperately trying to find. A detective from the San Francisco Police Department is on his way to help you. His name—Patrick Steele. In fact, he is probably at your house now. Before letting him in, ask for identification. I'll stay on the line until you hear the doorbell, and after you answer the door, and until you come back on the line and tell me you feel safe, and that Detective Steele is with you."

Chapter 28

York, Maine

IT WAS ALMOST MIDNIGHT. A breeze wafted through the open windows, stirring the humid air. Maria snapped off the TV, resting her head back on the couch. Another day and no leads as to Tabatha's whereabouts. She reached for her cell, hearing a ping that a text message was received.

Her brows shot up as she read the note: "We found her! Meet us. Tip room. Now! Liz ☺."

"On my way!" Jumping up from the couch, a fist pump in the air, grinning from ear to ear, she forwarded the text to Barly. Her cell pinged immediately: "Will join U at tip room!"

She raced to Stella's bedroom, calling out as she ran up the stairs. "Stel, Stel, wake up. Liz and Manny found Tabby."

Stella flung off the sheet, bolting out of bed in her kittens and puppies PJs. "No kidding? For real?"

"For real. Liz just texted me. I'm leaving right now to meet them at the tip room," Maria said, the pair dancing up and down in each other's arms. "Don't forget we're bringing Tommy home tomorrow."

"Not to worry. His room is all set. I guess the side-by-side cribs won't be empty for long. Now scoot."

"Bye, Stel. You're the best. I don't think I'll be long. Oh my God, It's almost one. I promise I won't wake you again ... well maybe—"

"I said scoot. Of course, you'll wake me—who said I'd be asleep?"

THE JEEP AND THE Mini Cooper screeched to a stop in the parking lot. Both drivers jumped out of their cars, the woman gleefully throwing her arms around the man, the man grasping her hand as they ran into the police department to join the two PIs.

Manny, his arm hanging around Liz's shoulder, listened to the voice coming from the speaker phone. They turned as Maria and Barly burst into the room. Exchanging hugs, Liz twirling, clapping her hands, as the voice continued from the speaker oblivious to the chaos on the other end.

Liz pulled Maria into a chair and then sat beside her. "Detective Steele, this is Liz. Hold on. The doctors who saved the baby and her brother just arrived. By any chance does Mrs. Thompson have a computer in the house with a webcam for Skype?"

Liz heard muffled voices and then Steele was back on speaker. "Yes. She said her late husband hooked it up but she hasn't used it. Give us a few minutes ... we'll call back."

While they waited for Steele, Manny ran to fix a fresh pot of coffee while Liz filled Maria and Barly in about the tipster's call. Manny hustled back in the conference room as Liz, listening to Steele's return call, was busy setting up a Skype account. Chief Roth joined them carrying a fresh carafe of coffee just as the laptop screen displayed a man and woman smiling back at them.

Liz finished up the tip story where she had left off, except now everyone was in a tight group watching the monitor. "Sorry about the noise, but your call is very exciting. Can you tell us again what you found at Diane Thompson's house?" Liz spoke in an even voice but was squeezing the life out of Maria's hand. The men were trying to look like they were above it all, but the excitement got the better of Manny, flinging his arm around Barly in a bear hug. Smiling, they sat on either side of the women, everyone staring at the two people on the screen—the man smiling, the woman with a sad face. She was going to lose her precious baby. Liz, unable to contain their good luck, planted a kiss on Manny's cheek.

"Of course. First, I'd like you to meet Diane Thompson. She's a bit shaken, but is cooperating fully."

"Hello. I'm Diane Thompson. I hope we can work together to put these awful people behind bars. Patrick, you tell them what you're going to do."

Liz and Manny exchanged grins. Diane had called the detective "Patrick." They had begun to bond. "She's pretty," Liz whispered.

"Hi again. Detective Steele here. Liz and Manny, can you introduce us to the doctors?"

"Yes, yes, Dr. Joe Bartholomew, but he's known as Barly, and Dr. Maria Grayson. Maria carried baby Tabatha out of the burning church and Barly carried her brother Tommy to safety. In back of us, you may not be able to see him, is Chief Roth, York Police."

"Okay, good. I checked the baby girl and the tip of her little toe, left foot, is gone. Diane has taken excellent care of the baby who's only been with her ... what, Diane?"

"About twelve hours since I picked her up."

"As I told Diane, we've been suspicious of the orphanage, Susan and Jeffrey Sinclair, for some time, but could never prove anything. I'm very happy to say, that has changed. Diane has agreed—"

"This is Diane. What Patrick is trying to say is that anything I can do so that no other adoptive mother has to endure what I've gone through, swindled by the promise of a baby to love, I'm willing to do."

"Diane, this is Maria. You are Tabby's guardian angel. We can't thank you enough for making the call. It must have been difficult. I know the grandparents, the Caldwells, will be forever grateful."

"Okay, folks, here's what I'm proposing. With Diane's help, the SFPD will set up a sting on the orphanage. We have to do this quickly before the Sinclairs' get suspicious."

"Detective Steele, Diane, this is Liz. Manny and I are flying to San Francisco on the next plane out of Boston, well, the next one after we get there, couple of hours—"

Barly reached for Maria's hand.

"Good. Both Diane and I think it's best that the baby leaves our jurisdiction as soon as possible. There is one stipulation, though. For the record, we have to match the baby's DNA—positive identification."

"This is Dr. Bartholomew. Manny will bring a DNA sample. Can you release the baby to him while the DNA tests are run?"

"Normally, no. But in this case, with Diane's consent, the baby already released to her care … so … well, I think she can let the little tyke take a vacation to Maine. Beautiful this time of year I hear," he said with a sly grin.

The group in the tip room let out a collective sigh, eyes darting one to the other. Liz nudged Manny, pointing to a spot on the monitor—Detective Steele's hand was protectively covering Mrs. Thompson's hand as the streaming video faded to black.

Chapter 29

———

THE STROLLER BUMPED ALONG over the cracks in the cement. With his thumb in his mouth, Tommy's eyes jumped from object to object in this fun place. The fumes belching from busses, vans, and a line of cars didn't seem to faze him. A roar drew his eyes up to a giant plane gaining altitude over his head.

Barly navigated the stroller through the sliding glass doors, Maria following close behind, the strap of a large tote over her shoulder. Barly nodded his head to the left fixing his sight on an open spot at the bottom of the escalator near the baggage-return carousels.

Standing out of the way of passengers as they rushed to meet friends or family, or simply darting to claim their luggage, the couple with a toddler in a stroller looked like a little family waiting to see a grandmother and grandfather riding down the moving stairs to greet them.

Barly stepped to the side of the stroller, placing a call on his cell and then a second. His conversations were short, returning to his duty—taking care of Tommy and Maria.

Tommy, mesmerized by so many noises, so many people, and a bell signaling a cart was coming through in the magic place, clamped down on his thumb. Maria smiled at him, trading glances with Barly who was grinning at the little guy. It was a miracle Tommy had a thumb left.

Suddenly, Tommy began jumping up and down in the stroller.

Maria looked up the escalator at a grinning redhead pressed to a large muscular man carrying a baby. Tabatha looked very small in Manny's protective arms.

The reunion was quick. Manny handed the sleeping baby to Maria, who in turn carefully placed the infant in Tommy's little arms but keeping a firm grip on her. Tabby opened her big blues for an instant seeing her brother, and then the fringe of long lashes fluttered shut returning her to dreamland, safe and sound.

With hugs, some tears, and quick thanks—a peck on their checks from Maria, a handshake with Barly—Manny and Liz ran for their connecting flight to Orlando, Florida. Liz, gripping Manny's arm so she wouldn't trip, her feet flying over the cement, turned and shouted over her shoulder. "I'll call. Have fun you two. Luv ya."

Maria called back, "I shipped your stuff. Love you, too."

Wiping a tear from her eye, Maria cradled Tabatha as Barly pushed the stroller. Relieved, their bodies relaxed, they walked at an easy gait to Maria's Mini Cooper. Barly opened the back door settling Tommy in his car seat, while from the other side Maria strapped Tabby into her new infant car seat. Taking out her camera, she shot a picture of Tabby, one of Tommy, and one of Barly leaning in the car giving Tommy's cheek a peck.

With Barly behind the wheel the Mini turned onto Interstate 95, North to Maine, and White Pines Memorial Hospital. The director requested the baby be returned to the hospital from where she was taken and then, after giving Tabatha a checkup, she would be released properly to the temporary caretakers. Other than the fact she had lost a half a pound, they found nothing amiss for her ordeal. Her little toe had healed over leaving a scant scar where the nail had been.

It was time to go home.

Before Maria left for the airport, Stella said she'd leave the light on. She was staying with Waldo along with a baying homesick Basset Hound, a litter of kittens, a couple of reptiles, a parrot, and various dogs and cats. She thought it would be fun, a trial run so to speak, but more important she wanted to give Maria and Barly some privacy with the kids.

Entering Maria's house Barly couldn't help but smile as he followed her, carrying a sleeping Tommy to his crib. The living room had an infant seat and a toddler's roll-around chair for Tommy. Passing the kitchen he noted two highchairs—one fitted with an infant carrier. The bedroom gave Barly a chuckle. Two cribs, two blowup mattresses between the cribs, and a doggie bed for Jenny. Maria and Barly had planned that the first night they'd keep the children together, and the two of them as well, to erase the anxieties of their separation.

It was late, almost eleven when Maria turned out the light, settling on the mattress next to Barly. Lying face-to-face, Barly reached for her hand and held tight. "It's been a good day, Dr. Grayson."

"I agree, Dr. Bartholomew." Maria shut her eyes, which instantly flew open. Sleep? Ridiculous! "Coffee, Dr. Bartholomew?" she whispered.

"Thought you'd never ask, Dr. Grayson."

Both in pajamas, they quietly tiptoed from the makeshift nursery, leaving the door ajar—just in case.

Barly slumped easily onto a kitchen chair, folded his hands behind his neck, stretching his bare feet out in front of him watching Maria position the filter, scooping dark-roast grounds, and pouring water into *Mr. Coffee*. Pushing the ON button she placed her hands on the edge of the counter staring down at the gurgling machine.

Barly got up, stepped to her, and circled her in his arms. "Hey, beautiful, everything is going to be okay."

Maria leaned her head back again his chest, his chin resting on the top of her silky auburn hair.

"You're wonderful with those kids, Barly. What's going to happen to them? My heart aches to be part of their lives, care for them, but my head says it's too soon."

Taking her hand, he guided her to a chair. "Sit. You're exhausted. I talked to the Caldwells while we waited for Manny and Liz at the airport. Brought them up to speed on Tabby, assuring them she was safe. They thanked me but didn't say anything else. I also told them that Tommy and the baby would be staying temporarily at your house. Maria, we both need time, now that the worry is over that Tabby might be hurt. I have a suggestion."

"What?" Maria asked, rising to pour the coffee. Barly retrieved her cream from the fridge setting the carton on the table.

"After the Caldwells I called my mother. She's spending some time at my cottage. Cooler on the lake than in the city. She wants to meet you."

Maria's brows rose. "I would very much like to meet her. Her paintings lining the walls in your cottage are so beautiful. She must be a beautiful person."

"Actually, that's what she's doing at the cottage—finishing a couple of paintings for an event at a Portland art show in mid September. How about we go up to the lake as soon as we can organize it? This weekend? Or the next? We can arrange coverage so we won't get called back for an emergency—unless it's something catastrophic. We'll have some quiet time to talk over what to do about the kids, get Mom's take on them. You know, a third party."

"How can we? We can't leave them now."

"I'll arrange for a couple of private nurses to stay here with the proviso that they aren't babysitters in the usual sense. That they have to spend time with them, play with them, tamp down any fears that Tommy might have that his baby sister is going to disappear again. Maybe we can convince Stella and Waldo to take a shift, maybe Harriett, too."

Maria sighed. "I don't know. Tabby's been through ... God knows what."

"You need a rest, Maria. You've been through so much the last few months—Mac, returning here, submerged in your residency work, and then the children. You need to get away." Barly got up, pulled her into his arms. He had to feel her lips on his. Now. She tasted sweet, fitting perfectly against him. He closed his eyes—this is how he wanted it to be with her, in his arms, feeling her heart beating against his. Leaning back, he was sure he saw love in her eyes. Love for him.

"A few days at the lake ... please say, yes, sweetheart."

Sweetheart. It was the first time he had called her that. Of course, she would say yes to his plans, and the sooner the better. "Can we go tomorrow?"

Barly hadn't expected her enthusiastic reply. With a smile, a lingering kiss, and a quick peck on her cheek, he returned their half-empty mugs to the sink laughing. "I think it will take a couple of days to get everything in place. I know you'll be a drill sergeant with the nurses—lists of instructions on how to care for the double Ts."

He caught her smile as she grabbed his hand and began leading him up the stairs to the dorm room. "I like that—double Ts. Now, let's you and I get some ZZZs. I have some serious lists to draw up in the morning."

Jenny was asleep on her doggie pillow tucked in the corner by a changing table. She much preferred to sleep between the cribs, but the mattresses were in her way so she divided her time at the foot of each crib and her own pillow.

Chapter 30

———

A SOFT BREEZE CIRCLED through the dorm room. Maria stuck her foot out from under the sheet. Her arms at her side, touching the carpeted floor, a smile spread across her face. It had been a beautiful day and the image of her and Barly lying side by side on the blowup mattresses between the sleeping children's cribs struck her funny bone.

Barly's hand reached for hers. Squeezed. The image heated up. She returned the squeeze and then rolled over on her side, her back to Barly. Thinking of his kiss before they climbed the stairs to their mattresses last night warmed her, delighting in the thought there was more to come.

Suddenly her brows shot up, blood draining from her face.

Looking up at Tabby's crib, hearing her soft breathing, an occasional sucking sound, Maria was struck by the enormity, the ramifications of what she had let herself begin to dream—she and Barly adopting Tommy and Tabatha.

Everything she wanted was in the shadows of this room, all within arm's reach—a baby and her brother, a father for them. A man, not any man—Barly—and the growing feeling for him racing through her. Growing? She could admit to herself that his making love to her in front of the fireplace at the lake house years ago had set her on fire, feelings she had immediately shut down. After all, there was Mac. She loved Mac, but not the kind of love that would endure. Not like what she felt for the man lying a few inches away.

She heard him turn on his side. His back must be next to her. She rolled over. She could touch him. No! This was too fast. She had learned not to trust her emotions where a man was concerned. But she had agreed to go to the lake, the cottage where the flame was ignited, and now fanned no more than a few hours ago.

Maria rolled over again, the sheet becoming entangled in her legs. She was going to meet his mother.

———

BARLY ROLLED AGAIN, KICKING the sheet from his legs. He could see Maria's shoulders in the moonlight. He wanted to crawl over the six-inch divide, curl around her. God, why did he have to go and kiss her? He was keeping his distance, waiting for her to come to him. But he was afraid that if she did come to him, she would suddenly retreat as before. He rolled again, the sheet tangling with his feet. He gazed up at Tommy in his crib. He could only see his little chubby hand next to the bars. Smiled at the occasional sucking sound. The thumb of his other hand was comforting him in his dreams.

Barly rolled again.

Maria's back was visible in the shadows. He had to admit he loved her, loved her from the moment they shared a glass of champagne on the deck of his cottage, snowflakes twinkling in her hair, the midnight kiss leading to the warmth of their touches, making love in front of the fire. God help him, he loved her more than he ever thought possible. He wanted her to be his companion for the rest of his life, his lover through all the years, his wife. But he was afraid to make a move. The kiss tonight showed him how easy it was to put his arms around her, to pull her against him, to put his lips on hers, to smell the sweet scent of her hair.

What was that? He listened.

Her breathing was even. She was relaxed, sleeping.

Barly quietly shifted his weight, rose from the blowup mattress, and tiptoed down the stairs. He had some serious thinking to do and he couldn't do it with her lying inches away.

Sitting at the kitchen table, sipping fresh coffee, he sensed her presence before she entered the room, stepping to the counter, pouring a mug of coffee.

Maria slid onto the chair at the table across from him. The early morning dawn picked up sparks of red in her sleep-tossed hair. Even without makeup, without brushing her hair in place, he thought she was the most beautiful woman he had ever seen. And, in his professional and private life, he had seen many.

Maria slowly raised her violet eyes. "How did you sleep?"

"Off and on, I guess you'd say. You?"

"Off and on," she said a grin lifting her cheeks, flushed with his being so close, as if they were a couple, lovers. "When do you want to leave for the lake?"

"I figure I can get my end in place by late this afternoon. If you find Stella and Waldo are willing to take the shift on the third day, just in case we get snowed in ..."

He smiled across at her, both of them remembering the blizzard on New Year's Day, the day after he held her in his arms ... in front of the fireplace. "If it all comes together, then I think we could fly up by three o'clock tomorrow, provided Tim is available to pick us up on such short notice, otherwise the next day. Allows us time to give the nurses instructions for the double Ts. Do you think Tommy will be afraid ... seeing us leave?"

"Barly, I'm as new to this as you are, but if we talk to him, tell him we'll be gone for three days, but then we'll be back for his dinner on day three ... maybe a calendar ... circle the day we leave and the one when we come back."

"God, Maria, he's only two. He's not an engineer in college. Harriett should be on deck first. He knows her. A kiss on his chubby cheek, see you in a little, should do it ... don't you think?"

"For a novice, you make a lot of sense. One change." Maria paused to sip her coffee.

"What's that?"

"We need the calendar. Circle the first day, leave two days in between, and circle the fourth day. *I* need the mind game so I think we have two full days."

"My mother will appreciate that as well."

"Do you think she'll be okay ... you know ... my coming along?"

"Hey, I told you she's eager to meet you."

Chapter 31

———

Moosehead Lake

THE SEAPLANE DESCENDED INTO a gentle glide onto the waters of Moosehead Lake, then taxied to Barly's dock. His mother stood watching from the deck of the cottage, hand to her brow shading her eyes from the brilliant sun reflecting off the water.

Barly thanked Tim as the pilot handed down two suitcases. "See you in three days," Barly called out over the noise of the plane's idling engines. "I'll call with the time."

Maria waved goodbye, turned and trekked up the path through the field of wild purple lupine, her eyes peeled on his mother. Even from a distance, Maria was drawn to her beauty as she stood next to her easel, a tray of paints mounted under the canvas.

As Barly approached the crest of the path, his mother disappeared into the cottage, reappearing at the front door, her blue painter's shirt splattered with crimson, yellow ocher, white, and a few specks of moss green. Her arms opened wide to receive him, placing her arthritic fingers on each side of his cheeks, her warmth cloaking around her son. "So good to see you. Now introduce me to this lovely woman behind you."

"Mom, I'd like you to meet Maria. Maria, my mother, Chenoa."

Maria stepped to Barly's side, Chenoa drawing her in to a warm hug. Holding Maria's shoulders, she leaned back. "Welcome, my dear. You have dominated every conversation I've had with Barly for the past few weeks, and now we meet. Please, come inside. Barly will tend to your bags. I understand you've been here before, several years ago. I'm set up in the loft's back bedroom so you take the front … the beautiful view of the lake. However, if you want more privacy we can swap."

Maria, overwhelmed by the aura of the Indian woman, finally found her tongue. "Mrs. Bartholomew—"

Laughing, the woman took Maria's hand, patted it. "Please, my dear, call me Chenoa."

"Chenoa, it's an honor to meet you and any sleeping arrangement you suggest is fine with me. Barly, you should have warned me of your mother's charm."

"Careful, she's been known to cast a spell on people. I'll take your suitcase up … front bedroom?"

"Yes, thanks." Maria's lips parted, but words failed.

"Mom, did the chef at the inn send the supplies I ordered? I don't know about you two girls, but I'm famished. A glass of wine anyone?"

"Sounds wonderful. Just give me a minute to freshen up." Maria turned to Chenoa, their eyes meeting, touched her arm, and then quickly mounted the stairs to the loft's front bedroom.

Chenoa turned to her son, nodding with a sweet smile. "Yes, your supplies were delivered. I'll be out front. The sun is hitting me in the eyes so I must pack up my easel. Wine on the deck?"

"Sounds right. Then we eat."

"Doesn't Maria have a dog? I thought she'd bring her for a nice romp in the woods."

"That was the plan, but when we left the house, Jenny trotted to her spot between the cribs and flopped down. Wouldn't budge from her post. Guard dog thing I guess."

———

THE AROMA OF COFFEE CIRCLED up to the loft. Maria's lashes batted once, then again. Yesterday had been wonderful. She sensed that Barly was disappointed when the neighbors down the road had dropped by. He was hoping for a walk around the lake. Rolling onto her back she stared up at the peak of the vaulted ceiling high above the A-frame cottage, allowing a view over the loft railing of the lake through the double tiered picture windows. Stretching her arms into the air, fingers laced together, she smiled, leaving the bed to dress. First she called to check on the kids. A nurse was on duty relieving Harriett—everything was running smoothly.

No one was in the kitchen but there was a note on the counter in Barly's handwriting. "Mom's painting on the side deck—something about the northern light was perfect this morning. Help yourself to coffee and join her. She's set up a chair. I'm running into town for more supplies. Back in a couple of hours."

With a mug of coffee in hand, Maria padded to the door in a white short-sleeved T over dark-green shorts and sneakers. A black-capped Chickadee was flitting from branch to branch in a nearby tree singing to another somewhere. Standing a moment in the doorway of the open slider, the morning air warm on her arms, she watched Chenoa paint.

Maria set her mug aside, retrieved the little red camera from her pocket and snapped a picture. Chenoa's black silky hair was held in a tight braid cascading down her back, a wave of bangs sweeping to the side of her brow. A floppy straw hat sat at an angle on her head keeping the sun at bay from her eyes but not shading the canvas in front of her.

Chenoa turned. "Good morning, dear. Sleep well?"

"Yes, thanks. Mind if I join you?" Maria picked up her mug, slipping the red camera back into her pocket.

"Please. There are some bagels and cream cheese on the counter. Lox in the fridge."

How pleasant the quiet morning, the birds singing, a few clouds dancing about overhead, sitting with Chenoa. Something about Chenoa calmed every breath Maria rhythmically drew.

"Chenoa, tell me about Barly's father. What kind of man was he? Barly did say he was a doctor."

"Barly told you his father died?"

"Yes. That must have been hard for you—beyond the fact that Barly was away at med school in New York. He never elaborated, seemed too painful for him to talk about his death."

Chenoa set her brush down and turned to look at Maria. Maria almost gasped at the beauty and wisdom in Chenoa's eyes, eyes of a light silvery blue. Barly's warm gray eyes must have come from her.

"I take it he hasn't told you about his demons."

"Demons?"

"Back then, my son hadn't decided what branch of medicine he wanted to specialize in, that is not until ... until his father died of a massive heart attack. Barly rushed home when I called telling him his father was taken to the hospital. But it took several hours to travel from New York to Portland. He was too late. Then and there he knew he wanted to be a cardiologist, but not any cardio doctor. He wanted to help others—in other cities, but all in the United States. Help people who didn't have the money to pay to heal a bad heart. He blames himself, feels to this day that if he hadn't vacationed, traveled abroad delaying medical school, he would have had the skill to save his father. Of course, he knows that wasn't possible ... the way it happened."

"When I was here before he told me about that dream to travel the country to help people, but he never said why."

"Did he tell you about Julie?"

"The patient he fell in love with in New York?"

"Yes. I believe he loved her, but ... this doctor-patient romance."

"Oh, I know well of that. I've often wondered if that was what I felt for Mac. Has Barly said anything about my husband?"

"Oh, my dear, he said nothing after you left York. My son ... well, my son fought off depression after you left as he did when Julie died. Again, like when his father died, he felt he should have been able to save Julie—you were a different matter. There was nothing he could do for you. You had to return to your life, the love you believed you had."

"How did you cope when your husband died?"

"Ah, the pain was great. I closed up the house in Portland and returned to my tribal family in Algonquin where I grew up. They healed me, wrapped me in familial love, healed the dove and then told me it was time to return to my life."

"Dove?"

"Chenoa means dove, my mother's little bird. I didn't think I could return to the house in Portland but I did. Several of the galleries booked shows featuring my paintings." Chenoa's eyes warmed holding the violet eyes filled with love gazing back.

"Your parents?" The violet eyes, filled with sympathy, knowing they must have passed on because there had been no mention of them.

"My father died a year ago and my mother soon after of a broken heart. No medicine can cure a broken heart. Now, Maria, please tell me about yourself. Barly says you've taken up photography as a hobby but you think you only take snapshots." Chenoa chuckled. "Another cup of coffee, dear?"

"Yes. Let me get it for you."

"Thank you, and perhaps a little something to eat—the bagels. I want to hear about the double Ts," she said smiling at Maria's reaction.

Yes, mother and son were close—double Ts!

———

SETTLING BACK ON THE deckchairs, with fresh coffee and bagels, Maria squinted at Chenoa. "Did Barly talk about my friends, Liz and Manny?"

"The private investigators?"

"Yes." Maria prepared a bagel with cream cheese and lox, handing it to Chenoa.

"When he called to tell me the trip to the lake was set, and the time I could expect you two, we chatted for quite a while. He told me about, the awful people at the orphanage ... honestly, their nerve thinking they could sell a baby ... told me how little Tommy—"

Maria pulled out her camera, flipped through some pictures, passing the camera to Chenoa. "Oh, he's adorable."

"The next one is Tabby."

"So sweet." Chenoa passed the camera back to Maria. "I believe you and Barly have a dilemma on your hands. Your hearts are pulled down many paths. You fear what might happen if you choose to follow any one of them."

"Yes, Chenoa. I can't make another mistake, can't take a chance on hurting Barly or the children."

"My dear, life is full of paths—you take one you follow another. How do you see yourself in five years, ten more? Is it alone? With a man ... Barly?"

"I've hurt people, Chenoa." Maria's face contorted into a blend of fear, regret.

"The past is done, Maria. Nothing you can do ... you were caught in circumstances you could not control. You must let those images go, deal with today. No path will be lined only with daisies. There will be thorns to pluck out. Love is bottled up in both you and Barly. You're afraid. Love has bitten you before. Bites that bled like bloody hell. Can you open your heart to giving, sharing, and accepting love? It all depends on what you see, Maria, looking through the lens to the future. The only thing for sure is that events will continue to skew the picture—one moment shedding the light of certainty for the path you're on, then plunging the path into darkness where you will be challenged to find your way again, testing your will. There will be many forks in the path ahead."

Maria glanced at the lake, swiped at a tear.

"Don't be afraid, Maria. Step through the lens."

Chapter 32

———

THE AIR REMAINED COOL with an occasional breeze even as the sun rose to its late-morning arc over the lake. Chenoa leaned her head back to catch its warmth on her cheeks. Her eyes clung to Maria standing at the rail of the deck staring at the crystals of light from the wake of a passing powerboat.

"How is your mother fairing, dear?"

Maria continued to stare at the water, her brows hitching up at the question. She was surprised Barly had mentioned Marianne to his mother. Yes, mother and son were obviously very close, sharing conversations with others. "She doesn't know me anymore." Maria turned back to Chenoa. Both their faces held pain in their eyes. "Alzheimer's is a hideous disease. I'm very thankful that she's being well cared for. But, I can't leave her there … alone. I've made some calls. I think I found a nice place in York where she will be treated well, and where I can visit. Maybe she'll come to think of me as a new friend."

"The past year has been difficult for you—your mother, your husband."

"Chenoa, how did you manage—your husband a doctor?"

"Looking back, it wasn't hard. Yes, I left my people, but many women in the tribe move, move all over the country. I was fortunate in that Portland was close by so I could visit my family. I met Barly's father at my first gallery show. Painting comes from the heart, filtering, interpreting what the eyes see. When I met Dr. Bartholomew my heart confirmed what I saw—I wanted to be with this man forever. Our lifestyles did not fight. Barly said your Mac was a fisherman—a demanding and dangerous profession. I imagine your lives must have clashed, been conflicted. Please excuse an old woman's ramblings."

Maria reached for Chenoa's hand, giving a gentle squeeze. "Not ramblings, wise words from someone with clear insight. You're right—our lives clashed. I wasn't prepared for how suddenly the differences bubbled to the surface. I knew of the potential incompatibilities. In some respects going into the witness protection program, far away from Florida, gave me time to evaluate my feelings. But, Chenoa, I disregarded my doubts of a patient-doctor affair. I was so alone—my mother receding into darkness. I wanted, needed Mac's love, desperately wanted to start a family which never came about. Chenoa, what do you think about adoption?"

"Adoption can be wonderful for the adoptive parents, if they are ready, and certainly can be a Godsend to the child."

"The two children that Barly and I pulled from the church fire … they're so precious. You should see Barly with little Tommy, the two-year-old."

"Barly, unlike you, is afraid of a family. Don't get me wrong, deep down I know he would like nothing more than to have a child—"

"Afraid? Of what?"

"Goes back to his feeling he failed his father, Julie, maybe even his strong attraction to you. Fear of failing you."

Maria shook her head, stepped back to the rail cradling the empty mug in her fingers.

In a brighter tone, Chenoa picked up her paintbrush, dipped it in yellow-ochre, touching it to the canvas. "Tell me about your hobby as a photographer?"

Maria laughed, a musical laugh at the thought of being called a photographer. "Well, I like snapping pictures, but I hardly—"

"Nonsense, my dear. The photo you *snapped* of my son chiseling his latest wood carving was beautiful." Noting Maria's raised brows, "Yes, he sent it to me."

"None of his carvings are here at the lake, or I haven't seen any if they're here."

"He says they aren't finished, aren't perfect. The two pictures of the double Ts are, as you say, precious. I know you've been snapping pictures here. Oh, yes, I caught you. You thought I was looking at my easel. I want to see more."

"Oh, no. I haven't culled out the bad ones."

"All right, but promise you'll *cull* out one for me before you leave. You can print a few on Barly's printer."

"What about my printer?" Barly asked, holding a wooden spoon with bits of garlic stuck on the side. He had returned from his trip into town and was now preparing their dinner.

"Just girl talk, son. What's the wonderful aroma coming from the kitchen? Another one of your famous pasta dishes?"

"That's the garlic. I'm trying something new for dinner."

"You must take Maria for a walk along the shore tonight. It's going to be a beautiful evening. One not to be wasted. I'll clean up after dinner."

"I agree about the walk but I know Maria will never let you clean up by yourself."

Chapter 33

IT WAS A BALMY NIGHT under the stars. Barly's arm relaxed around Maria's shoulders as they sauntered along the path cut through the woods—summer hiking, winter snowmobiling. So much to ponder, examine, weigh—her conversation with Chenoa, her feelings for Barly. Oh, so much more than feelings. An ache welled in Maria's core thinking of him, his arms around her, his eyes searching hers for answers.

"Chenoa and I talked while you were in town."

"And ...

"Yes, we talked about you, your father, my mother. I envy your relationship with your mother."

Barly pulled her into his arms, held tight, his hands combing through her silky hair, her soft scent teasing his brain. Lifting her chin, he kissed her warm lips gently, lingering, his heart pounding. Leaning away, he studied her eyes shining back into his. "Tell me what happened between you and Mac." His words were soft but insistent. He wanted answers.

She nodded, continuing down the path. Barly shoved his hands in his trouser pockets. He didn't know what she was going to say, but he had to find out so he could move forward putting her past behind him.

Maria inhaled the warm humid air filled with the scent of pine needles, the lush forest, the moonlight reflecting off the lake.

"When I found myself in York three years ago as a witness to murder, living a lie, torn from my life as I knew it to that point, I began to accept what I thought was love for Mac. It's said that separation makes the heart grow fonder, but separation can also twist what you think is real from something imaginary."

Maria paused, arms to her side, fingers clenched, images passing through her mind. Sighing, she looked up at Barly intent on what she was saying, waiting. No matter how painful it was to relive the years of her marriage to Mac, she had to continue.

"The man I witnessed murdering a patient was going to kill me, prevent me from testifying. The Feds, Agent Donovan, entered me into the Witness protection program. That night Maria Grayson died in a car crash, or so everyone was led to believe. Mac thought I was dead."

Maria glanced at Barly. His face gave nothing away. What was he thinking? Was she pushing him away? Feeling her chest constrict, she went on.

"It was almost a year before he learned I was alive, where I was, learned of my new identity—Dr. Morgan Grant. But not only did my name change, I had changed as well. No wonder our marriage didn't work ... it's clear now, but not then. Our lives were already on a collision course before I fled as a witness and then after we were married we didn't talk, couldn't seem to open up to each other. Shut down communication. I knew nothing of the rigors of commercial fishing. He didn't reveal to me the dangers he faced every day out at sea. Ah, yes, lack of communication—the worst symptom of a failing relationship."

The pain in her chest was building. The images painful.

"After we were married, the doubts I had dismissed before became real. Neither of us said anything. I dug deeper into my work, started training, specializing in pediatrics. The hours were long, spending most nights at the hospital. If I was home I was more often than not called back to the hospital. You know what a resident's life is like. The one very bright spot was the newborns. Caring for them I realized how lonely I was, how alone I was."

Maria stepped away from Barly. She looked to the heavens for an answer. Images of when she was a very young child.

"My mother told me when I started school, kindergarten, that my father had left her because he didn't want a baby, especially not a girl. She told me that I'd better make something of myself, prove him wrong. I became driven, a short marriage of convenience in med school—one apartment, two people pooling their meager funds. No love there. Then my patient, Mac ... I realized too late that what I felt was not love."

Barly reached out, touched her arm. Maria shook her head, waved his hand off. She wasn't finished.

"I began thinking that maybe a baby would bring Mac and I together. But nothing happened. Frustration set in. Our schedules didn't mesh, we avoided each other, always tired. Mac spent more time with his charter business, and netting shrimp most nights. We were incapable of breaching the void, the chasm grew between us."

Maria stood still, her arms tightened, trying desperately to hold her emotions in check. She turned to Barly, her face contorted in pain. She didn't see Barly, she saw Mac. Her eyes scanning his face.

"The day he was caught in the storm, killed by a shark, in the waters he loved more than anything, we quarreled—again I wouldn't be home when he returned. 'What kind of a marriage is this,' he yelled storming out of the house."

Gasping for air, Maria faced Barly in the shadow of the moonlight, her chest heaving as she relived the end of Mac's life. "I'm haunted by his words ... but ... even worse are the constant nightmares, the horror of Morgan Grant's last days."

Maria's eyes darted left then right. "I hid in the cellar, in the dark, the smell of mildew, a gun in my hand. Jenny leaned against me ... the man hired to kill me was in the house, upstairs, in the room overhead, calling to me, his voice soft, menacing, chilling, saying if I didn't come out he was coming after me. He pulled up on the hatch covering the opening to the cellar. I could see his shoes taking each step, silhouetted from the light behind him. Then I saw the gun in his hand, the barrel glistening. Still he came. I couldn't breathe. He started shooting. The bullets were ricocheting off the boulders of the cellar walls. I raised the gun. Shot. He fell to the floor. I heard his dying breath. I had killed the shadowy figure."

Maria gulped for air. Barly took a step but stopped. She was still in her nightmare. He had to let her continue.

"I called the police. I called Donovan. They came. The man I killed still lying in the cellar. Donovan said the man in the cellar wasn't the man I witnessed kill his rival in the hospital. Donovan was still there. Stella was there. A sting was setup with Stella and me as bait. It worked, the killer came into the house, started shooting at Stella and I, but Donovan had put blowup dolls on the couch. They withered and died from the killer's bullets. Agents stormed the house. Shot the man. He was bleeding. He was dead on the floor of my house. He had a wig on. He wasn't the killer. God, oh God, it was Stella's lover."

Maria stumbled to her knees but immediately gained her balance. Her words tumbling out, face distorted, fear gripping her.

"Mac came but the police wouldn't let him in the house. They let me go out to him. He pulled me into his arms in a car. A van drove up—oh, no, it's the albino, the man I saw kill his rival in the hospital, the man who had to kill me so I wouldn't testify. He and another man pushed Mac and I into the back of the van—drugged, unconscious. Now we're in the cabin of a boat, tied up. A terrible storm, the boat slamming down, wave after wave. Mac broke out of his ropes, freed me. We crept up the stairs onto the deck bouncing against the walls, the boat lurching. Mac overpowered the man at the wheel. The albino, the killer, was trying to reach me. He kept falling, terror in his pink eyes, hell bent on killing me. I grabbed a weapon, a gaff. He lurched for me. I drove the gaff into his neck. And then ... and then ..."

The words she had held from Barly had spilled out. She had told him everything. Everything as far back as when she was a baby. Hysterical, reliving the nightmares, her body shaking, tears flowing, gulping for air, she ran blindly, stumbling on vines, tripping on rocks. She turned, eyes staring at the man following her ... falling ... falling.

Barly grabbed her outstretched arms, her arms reaching out to him, but falling away.

Chapter 34

—

A BIRD'S SONG, A SUNBEAM painting a streak of light across the floor, across the quilt—a new day. Maria withdrew her hand from under the sheet tucked under her chin, her fingers touching her burning eyes. Barly had carried her back to the cottage, laid her on his bed. When she awakened during the night with fresh tears he had pulled her against him, stroked her hair until she fell back into a fitful sleep.

Rolling over she touched the dent in his pillow, the rumpled sheet where he had slept. She was still dressed in the jeans and white T-shirt she wore last night when they went for a walk in the moonlight.

With a soft knock on the door Barly tiptoed into the room carrying two mugs of coffee. He smiled in response to her open eyes. "You're awake. How do you feel?" His voice was soft, caressing. He sat on her side of the bed as she slowly scrunched up, leaning back against the cherry headboard. His eyes scanned her face for signs of pain hoping they passed during the night.

"Drained, weak."

"Take a sip of coffee," he said touching her swollen eyes.

"I must look awful."

Barly tucked a piece of auburn wave behind her ear. "You look beautiful, at peace."

"I … I'm sorry, I … last night …

Barly shook his head. "Don't be sorry, sweetheart. Everything you've been through … you bottled it all up inside. It's a miracle you had the strength to show up at the hospital. I'm guessing your patients were your lifeline. Trust me, Maria. I'm one of the good guys. I promise I won't hurt you."

Maria's eyes traced his face—smooth shaved chin, warm gray eyes behind the black-rimmed glasses. He looked like he was dressed in white scrubs, his version of casual attire—muscular arms and bare feet the coloring of his mother's olive skin, a contrast to the soft white cloth of the pants and T-shirt. She nodded, unable to speak, tears forming. Her lashes batting to hold them at bay. She understood he was one of the good guys. His thumb wiped away one tear that spilled on her cheek.

They smiled at each other, nascent love revealed in their eyes, love too fragile to risk saying something that would halt the bloom of their feelings.

Barly's cell rang. Pulling it from his pants pocket, he checked the caller ID. "It's Stella," he said handing the phone to Maria.

"Hi, Stel, Are the kids okay?" Maria glanced at the clock. It was ten. She raised her brows to Barly with a shake of her head. She had never slept so late.

"They're fine. You weren't answering your phone so I called Barly's number. Can you hold it to his ear or something?"

"Sure. You sound upset. What's wrong?"

"Well, I'm not sure. There's a woman … standing in front of me. She says she's Tabatha's and Tommy's aunt … their mother's sister. She's demanding I release the children to her."

Chapter 35

WITH STELLA'S WORDS RINGING in their ears, an aunt demanding to take the children, and aware the aunt was standing beside Stella, Barly calmly, but firmly, directed Stella not to relinquish Tabby and Tommy under any circumstances.

Maria nodded in agreement.

"Stella, Maria and I will be back in York ... about four hours. Tell the woman to leave ... come back after the children's guardians return. Threaten her that you'll call the police chief if she doesn't leave. Oh, and ask her for identification. A driver's license. Get the number of the license plate. Better yet, scan a copy on Maria's printer. You know how to work it."

Maria pulled the phone closer so she could talk. "Command Jenny to stay by the kid's cribs. Use the teeth command—that'll make her back off."

"I don't have to tell Jenny. The only time she's left their room was to go outside to relieve herself, eat a few mouthfuls of food from her dish, a slurp of water, and then races up the stairs to the cribs, or wherever they are."

Maria rolled her eyes at Barly. "Okay. Bye."

Barly slapped the phone shut. She didn't need this, but life has a way of intruding.

Maria leaned into him with a soft reassuring kiss on his lips—*I'm okay*. Scooting to the other side of the bed, standing to test her legs, she hurried to the loft to shower gaining strength with each step, strength returning to her legs as she pictured the children— threatened again. Packing, she heard Barly instructing Tim to pick them up as soon as possible. There was an emergency in York.

Chenoa, overhearing her son's conversation, started a fresh pot of coffee for a thermos while preparing bacon, egg and cheese bagels for their return flight to York.

Maria, her suitcase thumping down the steps, reached for the fresh coffee Chenoa held out to her, brows raised. "The children ... a woman says she's their aunt and is demanding my friend release them to her."

Chenoa pulled her into an embrace, exchanging glances of concern. Maria turned stepping quickly to Barly's small study. Culling through the pictures on her camera, she selected one, printing it in grayscale.

"Maria, Tim's at the dock. Are you ready?" Barly called out grasping her bag in the doorway of the kitchen.

"Go to the plane, son. Maria will be with you in a minute. She went to your office for something." Chenoa turned away, her hand pressed against her chest.

"Mom, what's the matter?"

"Just a little indigestion."

"Hope my cooking wasn't that bad—a little spicy maybe." Barly hugged his mother. "I love you. I'll call."

Maria joined Chenoa as Barly disappeared out the door. "Here, my dear, a little something for the plane. You need to eat—your eyes look tired. Come back soon. Will you?"

"Yes, Chenoa. I'm so glad we had yesterday ... take care of yourself. Here's your picture. I think it's the best one ... but I didn't get a chance—"

The black and white portrait brought tears to Chenoa's eyes—the lighting, the intense look on her face. Her arthritic fingers holding the tip of the paintbrush to the canvas. She had looked up just as Maria snapped the camera.

———

THREE HOURS AFTER STELLA called, the small plane returned to York, landing on the unmanned airstrip. Thanking Tim, Barly grabbed the handles of the suitcases, transferring them to the trunk of his Jeep. As Tim's plane took off gaining altitude, Barly turned onto the road heading to Maria's house. They had no idea what to make of the woman, but one thing was for sure, she was going to be grilled for information before any discussion of transferring the children to her care took place.

Pulling her cell from her tote, Maria tapped the directory, looked up at Barly then out the windshield. "Hi, Liz. Barly and I need your help ... I think."

"The connection is scratchy, Maria. Call back if the line drops. What's up? You sound ... nervous, or something."

"We just flew back from the cottage. Stella called. A woman came to my house demanding Stella hand over the children to her. Says she's their aunt. That's all I know, but I may be calling after I talk with Stel. Maybe you and Manny can find out if she's legitimate."

"We'll be waiting to hear from you, Maria. Is the woman still at the house?"

"No. Stella told her to leave or she'd call the police. Told her to come back this evening when the children's guardians were home. She made a copy of the woman's driver's license."

The signal dropped. Maria pocketed her cell as Barly turned into her driveway. Stella opened the front door and Jenny shot out, raced down the walkway, sat panting, tongue hanging out in front of her mistress. She barked, whined, and then raced back into the house.

Barly exchanged smiles with Maria. "That's some dog. We should deputize her as the kids' permanent guardian."

After transferring the bags from the car to the house, they took a quick peek into the kid's room where Jenny was lying with her head on her paws, her eyes following Barly and Maria as they each checked the cribs, kissing the napping children's heads. Tiptoeing out of the room, they returned to the kitchen where Stella waited with a pitcher of iced tea.

"Here's the copy of her driver's license. North Carolina. The photo is definitely the woman who came here."

"Describe her, Stella," Barly said. "Everything you remember about her."

"Okay." Stella looked down at her glass as Maria poured tea over ice into glasses for Barly and herself.

"She's about my height—five feet, maybe an inch more. Probably in her thirties. Blonde, as you can see from her picture. Nervous, but very demanding, like I said on the phone. She didn't say anything more other than she was the kid's aunt. She didn't know where her sister was. Insisted that the kids should be with family. Name on the license is Jane Flintrock."

Maria turned to Barly. "Can you call the grandparents, see what they know about an aunt?"

Barly stepped out the back door, cell to his ear.

Maria flipped open her phone and punched Liz's number. "Okay, Liz. This is what we have so far. Her name is Jane Flintrock. Hold on a second. Stel, can you email a copy of the license to Liz? Her card is on my desk with the information. Liz, you'll have a copy shortly. Hang on. Barly wants to talk to you."

"Hi, Liz. I just talked to the Caldwells, the kids' grandparents. They don't know of any aunt, but of course they really know nothing about their son's wife or her family. Didn't know the maiden name of Stevie's wife. Never heard their son mention the name Flintrock. Crazy name, they probably would have remembered if they'd heard it. So, no help there. Liz, you and Manny heard most of this when the Caldwell's came to the hospital."

"Yes. You're on speaker so Manny heard what you told me. He asks if you can send us an email with what you just said so we have spellings, yada yada. Manny just printed the email from Stella. He has a connection from his days as Daytona Beach Police Chief, Criminal Investigation Division, with a captain at the Quantico Marine Base. He'll call you guys as soon as he has any information on Stevie's wife—last name, sister thing, yada yada."

Chapter 36

―――

York, Maine

CARS WERE PARKED FENDER to fender in the tiny parking lot at The Crab Shack. Hungry, disgruntled patrons, wiping sweat from their faces, jockeyed in line to place their orders, then stood smooshed together waiting for their number to be called. Finally, with foam boxes in hand, they darted to the picnic tables squeezing into tiny spots between the slim and fat, young and old, heartily attacking lobster, fried clams, or hot dogs in bulky rolls.

Everyone had peeled down to shorts, tank tops, and flip flops with the heat … everyone except for the old. Their feet were stuffed in sneakers and short-sleeved shirts over long pants.

Floyd, a triumphant grin on his face, joined his girlfriend, a babe he had long admired and hoped, if luck would have it, to marry in a few days. Janie smiled at him, turning her back on the beefy man who sat next to her with his anorexic wife.

Straddling the picnic bench, Floyd kissed Janie's mustardy lips and then took another bite of his own hot dog smothered with onions, relish, and ketchup.

"What's our next move, baby doll? I don't mind this hick town as long as we can have dogs like this, but I'd like to get on with our little caper. Did you see the kids?"

"No, I told you, Floyd, the babysitter wouldn't let me near them. Gave me a start, I tell you, when this monster dog snarled at me from the top of the stairs. The sitter called a couple of docs, said they were guardians of some sort. Probably the ones you circled in the newspaper. Of course, I put on the indignant act, that I was the kid's aunt just like we planned. She said to come back later—tonight."

"I like that. Let her know you're not to be put off. You mean business."

"Damn right I mean business." Janie leaned into Floyd, licking a smear of ketchup off his upper lip, giggling.

"What's so funny?" Floyd raised his brows, his tongue crossing over his mustache.

"You tickle me. Back to plan *A*. You circled the article in the newspaper that the father had died and the mother's whereabouts was unknown, right? I want to get the story straight." Janie took a sip of her extra large coke.

"Right. There was another article a few days later that the grandparents came to the hospital and returned home immediately to North, or was it South Carolina? Doesn't matter. The point is they didn't want them. You're sure Trixie isn't going to give us any problem?"

"Nah, she doesn't want anything to do with the screamers. Complains that all day they either cry or poop. Sometimes both at once. She's sick of 'em. However, once we pull this off, you and I will disappear so she can't get into the act. And, Floyd, that was in North Carolina where my friend Trixie lived." Janie opened her eyes wide, shaking her head at Floyd's stupidity.

"Oh well, I figure we'll get us appointed as foster parents, get the cash flowing, then start on you adopting them—you being family, saying you're the aunt and all. Once that happens, the gravy train will just keep rolling—money from good old Stevie's military benefits for his kids," Floyd said.

"I'm a little surprised the Caldwells haven't taken them." Janie glanced at the line of cars stalled waiting for a van of loudmouths trying to back out of the little parking lot.

"Why? You said you never met them. Only Trixie called them bores the way they doted on Stevie. Didn't pay any attention to her. Still, they may be willing to help pay for the kids support being we will be taking them off their hands. We want to get as much money coming our way as we can from the little poopers."

"Floyd, once we get the kids, you said we'd get married. We'll be a real family."

"You bet, baby doll. Spotted a little chapel in town … a real family with a steady income. I love you, Janie."

"I love you too, Floyd."

The two kissed mixing yellow mustard with red ketchup.

"Do you want me to come with you tonight, Janie?"

"Not this time. Besides, fang dog may not like you. If I have any trouble, like the docs throwing barbs at me—single-parent stuff, then maybe tomorrow a potential uncle, my handsome fiancé, can come on the scene." Janie said, wiping a smudge of ketchup off Floyd's chin.

"You are so smart, Janie. Asking Trixie for that family information. She never asked you why you wanted it?"

"Never. Said she was shedding her past for good, laying it on me. Of course, I happily accepted her take on the situation. Actually, I thought about dating Stevie once. I don't know if he said anything to his parents, but I'm going to play it up that I loved him, felt awful when Trixie ran off … that he was trying to find her to get a divorce and marry me. That should make everyone feel better."

"Hey, Janie, what about me? You sayin' you wanted to marry him doesn't make *me* feel so good."

"Floyd, come on … now, I love you. You're my protector. We want to be a family … I can even say that you remained by my side just in case Stevie-boy didn't get a divorce. That's how much my Floyd loves me. Of course, I won't bring your name into the conversation unless I have to show I can provide a stable home."

Floyd scowled. Why would Janie say such things?

"Hey, my handsome fiancé, stop with the long face. It's all just a story, except the part where you found a chapel. I'm anxious for that part to happen."

"Well, okay. Do you think you'll come back to the motel with the kids tonight?"

"Depends on the hick docs. If they're tired of taking care of them. After all they did take off for who knows how long, then maybe. Did the motel manager say he has cribs?"

"No problem. But he said, stern to my face, that we could only stay one night if they cried disturbing the people next to us. That's why he switched us to an end unit."

Chapter 37

——

IT WAS A RACE against time.

Jenny stood guard in the kitchen. Tommy was corralled in a playpen. Tabby sat on the floor in a large infant carrier next to the playpen. The dog and the two little people were mesmerized with the new game the big people were playing.

Cribs, bedding, the extra highchair that Tabby was going to grow into, along with duffle bags filled with disposable diapers, little clothes in different sizes, and toys were hauled out to Waldo's van—an operation executed with military precision. Maria and Barly, Stella and Waldo were hiding the children at Barly's house.

"This is kind of exciting, Maria. Stealth like. Right, Waldo?" Stella said handing the chain of stuff from Maria up to Waldo.

"I guess. Remind me never to cross you girls."

The women dashed back into the house—Maria grabbing Tabby, Stella whisking Tommy out of the playpen. The men stashed what was left in the kitchen into the back of the van. Waldo slammed the doors shut, climbed behind the wheel next to Stella, and backed out of the driveway waiting for the Jeep to take the point position.

Barly and Maria led the procession through the streets of York. The white van—*Doc Whistle's Pet Clinic, Nails to Tails*--painted with dogs, cats, birds, scaly reptiles, and a couple of turtles—following close behind.

Backing into Barly's driveway, two of the three garage doors opened, and the process of fifteen minutes ago was played out in reverse. Jenny raced into the woods for a quick stop before rejoining the game. She returned in time to escort Tommy into a new kitchen.

"Tommy, you go with Stella. She'll give you some Cheerios while Waldo and I put up the cribs. Maria, need any help with Tabby?" Barly called out.

"I'm good." Maria banged into the door frame with Tabby in the infant seat, joining Stella waiting for Waldo to bring in the highchair. Stella exchanged grins with Maria setting Tommy on the floor.

"Hurry up you two guys. Get the cribs ready so we can put the double Ts to bed," Stella said rooting around a bag of baby food for the little box of Cheerios.

Jenny, tongue hanging out, flopped down on the kitchen's braided rug next to Tommy, head down on her paws, eyes darting as the humans continued the game, rushing in and out of cars and through doors.

Barly returned to the kitchen, swiping two of Tommy's little Cheerios rings. "Cribs are up."

"You two go on back to the house. That Janie Flintrock person could show up early and you don't want to tip your hand that the kids are out of her reach. Go on, scoot. Isn't that right, Tommy, my man? Wait, the bedding." Stella scooped Tommy up from the floor sliding him expertly into the highchair where he immediately began stuffing his mouth with the ringy cereal.

Tabby, not wanting to be left out, began to cry, but Stella, by now an expert, gently popped the nipple of her nighttime bottle into her puckered lips. Satisfied that the screams were stifled, Stella stood with her hands on her hips smiling at her little charges.

Laughing, Waldo left the kitchen to help Barly, passing Maria in the hall relieving her arms of the bedding.

"You'd better be careful, Waldo," Barly said pulling up the side rail of Tabby's crib. "Stella looks like a natural."

"She does doesn't she. Maybe I'll have to do something about that. Soon." Grinning, he took the crib sheets Barly handed him.

Maria's eyes crinkled in the corners. "Thanks, Waldo. We'll be back as soon as we finish with the aunt."

BARLY BACKED THE JEEP out of his driveway, careful not to nick Waldo's zoo-van. Reaching over for Maria's hand just as her cell rang, he grabbed the brake handle instead.

"Liz, perfect timing. The children are at Barly's and we're heading back to my house. Janie what's-her-name should be arriving in less than hour. Speak up so Barly can hear. He's driving a little crazy so I'll put you on speaker."

"Can you hear me now?" Liz asked with a giggle.

"Yes. Go ahead." Barly said checking the rearview mirror. He was driving over the speed limit.

"Manny and I have tons of info for you. Just sent you an email. Manny came up big time from his Quantico contact. Seems his friend had served with Stevie, met the missing wife a couple of times, and in the words of Stevie's buddy, 'He'd do everything in his power to keep the little ones from the clutches of the fake aunt.'"

"Fake aunt?"

"Fake as a crocodile imitating a rattlesnake. The guy had Sergeant Steven Caldwell's record on his computer faster than Manny could take a sip of coffee. Wife's maiden name is Trisandra Flintrock becoming Trisandra Caldwell when she married Stevie. Stevie's buddy said she uses the name Trixie Doll when she sings with a band. Kind of a cute stage name, don't you think?"

Maria rolled her eyes at Barly.

"Now, things get a little complicated. Manny dug into Trixie's pedigree. She was married the first time to a Cory Unger. That's when she had Tommy. Then she married the Caldwell guy and had Tabatha. Anyway, Trixie gave birth to a baby girl at a hospital in Raleigh. We found that Trisandra Flintrock-Unger-Caldwell's parents live in the same city. And, here's the kicker. Trisandra is the Flintrock's only child. AKA, the aunt is a fake."

"Wow, we owe you big time."

"Give us a week at Barly's cottage—Moosehead Lake isn't it?"

"It's yours whenever you want," Barly said with a quick grin in Maria's direction.

"Wait ... good idea ... Manny wants to know if you'd like him to talk to his buddy Roth, the York Police Chief. When you and Mac, sorry I didn't mean to bring up his name, anyway when you were rescued, they became buddy-buddy like. Now a fake aunt, yada

yada … I'm rambling, I'm so excited. Anyway, Manny could call him, fill him in, and say that you might be calling for his help. Maria, it would be quite a reception for Janie Flit-whatever, if the police were there to arrest—"

"Arrest?"

"Oh, yeah. We found Miss Jane Flintrock in the North Carolina, criminal division database. Real name is Jane Wolf—the driver's license she gave Stella is phony. She has a record. A looong record. Mostly petty stuff, but did spend a year in the slammer. Seems she hooked up with another criminal, Floyd Hackworth."

Maria and Barly laughed so hard tears came to their eyes. "Come on, Liz. Hackworth? Flintrock and Trixie Doll?" Maria said.

"Stage names, kiddo. Or maybe they plan to write their memoirs. Anyway, Manny just hung up with Chief Roth. Says he's standing by in case you need him."

Chapter 38

———

ARMED WITH THE INFORMATION from Liz, Maria called Chief Roth. The Chief felt it wise to attend the meeting with Miss Jane Flintrock, a woman with a record in North Carolina. He arrived with Detective Rodney Hall, who parked the squad car out of sight in Maria's garage. The undercover detective would facilitate the taping of Jane's story and if necessary, her arrest. Chief Roth was set up to monitor the meeting from Maria's computer room.

Nine o'clock rolled around and no Jane Flintrock.

Maria topped off the three mugs of coffee. "Maybe she's not coming. If she's a fraud we may have scared—"

The doorbell's ding-dong chimed.

Three heads jerked up, eyes darting one to another. As planned, Maria and Barly were wearing a wire, recording everyone's words. Also, Rodney, dressed in jeans and a white polo shirt, would hang back—a friendly neighbor who just happened to drop by. Maria was to answer the door—female to female—less intimidating. Roth wanted Jane Flintrock to be as relaxed and gabby as possible—he was monitoring the kitchen conversation from a bug stuck under the kitchen table.

Maria stood, stroked her tan capris, and walked to the front door. Barly and *the neighbor* remained at the kitchen table.

"Hello, Miss Flintrock?"

"It's Ms. Flintrock, I'm not a teenager you know."

"Of course, you're not. I'm Dr. Maria Grayson. Come in. I thought maybe you'd changed your mind. Dr. Bartholomew and I were just having a cup of coffee. Follow me. We have some concerns which I'm sure you can clear up."

Jane followed Maria to the kitchen. Seeing the two men, her eyes switched from one man to the other.

"Hello, Ms. Flintrock. I'm Dr. Bartholomew. Won't you have a seat?"

"Who's he?" Jane pointed to the other man leaning against the counter.

"This is Rodney, my neighbor. He knew I was away and stopped by to ask how I liked Moosehead Lake. He's looking for a vacation spot. Coffee, Jane?" Maria asked as Rodney nodded hello to Jane.

"No thanks. Tell me your concerns. I want to take the kids tonight. We're heading back—"

"We?" Maria stepped to the cupboard for another mug which she placed with a cream pitcher in front of Jane who sat down at the table across from Barly.

"I guess maybe I will. Do you have any sugar?" she asked pouring a good dose of cream into the coffee.

Maria retrieved the sugar bowl and a spoon setting them on the table and then took a seat beside Jane.

"My boyfriend … fiancé, loves kids and is very happy that we'll start married life with a complete family—boy and a girl." Smiling sweetly at the neighbor, she added two teaspoons of sugar to the now very thick concoction in her mug. "You might like to know that I was madly in love with Stevie. Heartbroken when he married Trixie. That's why I practically feel like I'm already the kids' mother."

"Oh, I didn't know about your plans. Dr. Bartholomew, I think we should meet … What's his name, Jane?" Maria said.

"Floyd. He's wonderful. Always looking out for me."

"I once knew a Floyd," Rodney helped himself to a spoonful of sugar. "Hell of a guy. What's your Floyd's last name?" he asked flashing a disarming smile at Jane.

"Oh, Rodney, wouldn't that be something? The Hackworth's are very big in Raleigh. That's where I'm from."

"Floyd Hackworth?" Rodney, returning to his relaxed stance next to the counter, grinned at Maria.

"Jane, you said 'we're leaving.' Where's Floyd. I really have to meet him if he's going to be the father—"

"Oh, he's just up the street. Didn't want to horn in on our negotiations."

"I'll go find him, ask him to join us for coffee. Or, maybe something stronger for us men. Right, Dr. Bartholomew?" Rodney said.

"Sounds good to me, but Maria and Jane might like to join us for a little drink," Barly said.

Barly pushed his chair back. "How about some of that red wine you have, Maria? Six-pack of beer still in the fridge?"

"Rodney, you go get Floyd while I put out the glasses. Jane, wine or beer?" Maria winked at Rodney as he turned to leave.

"Wine, please. Floyd always buys beer, so, I'll go with the wine," Jane said.

"Do you know where your sister is, Jane? What's her name again?" Maria handed the wine bottle to Barly along with a corkscrew.

"I told your babysitter this morning that I don't know where Trixie is. Her real name is Trisandra. Trisandra Flintrock. That was before she married the Caldwell guy. She's my best friend, like forever ... as well as my sister. We used to go to the bars together. She played chaperone being a year older than me. I tried, but I couldn't find her, so I know she'd want me to take care of her kids. She trusts me ... trusted me. I'm their aunt, family for God's sake. Grandparents should be indebted to me for taking them off their hands, taking care of them. If they don't give us support then we'll sue them for help."

The front door banged shut, footsteps hustled over the pine floorboards to the kitchen.

"Here we are. Two thirsty guys. Where's that beer you promised, Dr. Grayson?"

"Coming right up. You must be Floyd." Maria offered her hand. Floyd pumped it twice and then Barly's.

"Hello, Floyd. I'm Maria's friend, Dr. Bartholomew, and you've met our neighbor Rodney."

"Yessiree, I have." Floyd took the chair that Barly pulled up to the table. Nodded thank you to Maria for the beer.

"Well, Floyd, Jane says you and she want to be parents. Start out with a complete family she said. How are you going to take care of the children?" Maria asked. "Are you both going to work?"

Jane piped up. "Oh, I'm going to be a stay-at-home mom. As I said, Stevie and I were in love. That's what he would want. Floyd is a mechanic. Not just any old mechanic. He's the head guy at the shop, of one of those big chains. Keeps our car running like ... like I don't know what. I just know it never stalls. But who knows what we'll do. We're talking about both of us retiring, what with Stevie's military pay for his surviving children now that he's passed on. Never like to say somebody's dead. Passed on sounds like he's passed on but looking down. You know, watching that his kids are well taken care of."

"Trixie is lucky to have you as a sister, isn't she Floyd?" Rodney said.

"She sure is." Floyd scowled hitting Jane's leg with his knee.

"Floyd, stop that. I told you about Stevie. Now, you're my man."

"Are you still at that car place, Floyd? Must be a hell of a great place to work ... all that equipment you can use to keep your car, what was it you said, Jane? Keep the car humming with all those parts?" Rodney said.

"Janie didn't say it quite like that but you're right. The boss says he's lucky to have me—I'm so good. Lets me take what I want."

The doorbell chimes played for the second time.

"Now, who can that be?" Maria said setting her wine glass on the table.

"I'll get it." Barly winked at Maria, setting his bottle of beer on the counter.

Opening the front door, he took a double take. A pair of punk rockers stood facing him. "Something I can do for you two? Car trouble?"

The young woman, black hair—purple streak on one side orange on the other, holding a large black cat—inched forward. The young man with her, black Mohawk on top of his blonde curls circling his shoulders, shifted from one foot to the other.

The woman, her black T-shirt emblazed with: *A Guy and a Doll*, spoke. "I'm looking for a Dr. Grayson or a Dr. Bartholomew."

"I'm Dr. Bartholomew."

"Swell. I'm Trixie Doll."

Chapter 39

"TRIXIE DOLL. WELL, isn't that a coincidence. Come on in. You, too ... what's your name?"

"He's George Guy, like in a guy and a doll. He takes care of me, so no messing around, Dr. B. If you know what's good for you that is."

"Wouldn't think of it."

Trixie sashayed through the door around Barly, motioning for George to follow, her sandals smacking her heels with each step. "Where can we talk, Dr. B?"

"In the kitchen, around the corner. The others will be surprised to see you I expect."

"Others?"

"Trix? Oh, my God. Trix, what are you doing here?"

"Janie, imagine finding you here. Oh, that's right, you were going to collect my kids ... among other things."

"Hi, Floyd. Can I have some of your beer?" George said.

"Wait, I'll get you one," Maria said her eyes bugging out at Barly. "Rodney, can you get a couple of chairs for our guests—*from the computer room?*"

"Yeah, sure, Dr. G." Rodney was grinning like a Cheshire cat or more like the big black piece of furry animal Trixie was carrying. This assignment was getting more fun by the minute.

"Trix, what the hell is going on?" Janie asked.

Trixie's cat stretched up its back then settled down, spilling over her lap.

"Trix, beer? Wine?" Maria asked.

"Yeah, sure. Wine. Just protecting my interests that's all, Janie dear. Where are my sweet babies anyway?"

"We were just discussing them with Jane and Floyd." Maria handed a glass of wine to Trixie and a cold beer to George who immediately twisted off the cap, downing several guzzles.

"Trix, have you changed your mind? You and George, taking—"

"No, no. They're yours, *sis*. Just a slight change to the arrangement. I'll collect the widow's benefit along with the money for the care of Stevie's and my children. You can still do the nurturing. But I'll pay you from Stevie's benefit package."

"You bitch. That was not the agreement," Janie yelled, jumping to her feet, hands on her hips, glaring at Trixie.

"Don't you call me a bitch, you little fraud," Trixie screamed in return, rocketing out of her chair, hands balled at her side ready to strike. The black cat hissed as it landed on the floor immediately saving her humiliation at being dumped, by grooming her long furry tail.

Everyone, now standing, pushed their chairs back clearing the ring for a fight.

The doorbell chimed for the third time but nobody moved.

Rodney stepped into the kitchen with two folding chairs as Chief Roth walked through the door, waving to Barly and Maria that he would answer the bell.

"Who was that?" Janie shouted.

"A friend taking a look at my computer," Maria said.

Roth, an imposing six-foot figure, a holster-belt high on his hips loaded with a couple of guns, strolled into the kitchen with his uniformed officers, also armed with guns, and cuff links. Roth, stern look on his face, was smiling inside. He hoped the firepower would get the gang of four to cooperate, turn on each other. Roth and his men definitely had their attention when they sauntered into the kitchen. Roth, arms crossed over his ample chest displaying the gun belt under his jacket, spoke to the group.

"Tell you what, Ms. Trixie Flintrock and Ms. Jane Wolf, *you and your boyfriends* are going to take a little ride with these nice officers down to the station. Yes, we know all about you, Miss Wolf, and, we know that Ms. Trixie here doesn't have a sister. There are several things that don't exactly correlate with the truth. That way, at the station, we can sort all of this out. Oh, but Miss Wolf, you'll be spending at least the night as our guest ... maybe more."

"Oh yeah. For what? I ain't done nothing wrong."

"Well, fraud and extortion will do for starters. And you, Ms. Trixie, I wouldn't be looking to take the children anytime soon, beings how you said you don't want them, but more important, being a party to fraud. We caught everything on tape little ladies. But, Trixie, Trisandra Caldwell, you should have checked with the military. Sgt. Steven Caldwell died while on active duty so you are eligible to some benefits as his widow, as well as benefits for his children. Of course that will all have to be determined, especially after you stated, for the record, that you didn't want the children. I can set up a meeting for you with an Army Officer if you like."

Trixie scowled at Roth. "Yeah. I'd like," she muttered.

"Hey, why do I have to go to the police station? This was all Janie's idea." Floyd plopped down on a chair frowning at Janie.

"Me either. I just drove Trix here." George flopped down on a chair beside Floyd.

"Well, boys, let's just say we need to figure out how deep into this conspiracy you are. You know … accomplice stuff. Detective Rodney Hall, why don't you read them their rights. That way you don't have to repeat it four times. Oh, and Ms. Flintrock, I'd keep that cat on your lap. Dr. Grayson has a vicious dog."

Roth and the uniforms hustled the conspirators out the door, Roth rolling his eyes at Maria as he pulled the door shut behind him turning off the diatribe—Janie and Trixie sputtering their innocence, threatening they would have their jobs, and threatening Dr. G that she would be seeing their lawyer with a court order to hand over the children.

"I guess that's our clue to go home and relieve our babysitters," Barly said draping his arm around Maria's shoulders.

Home? Our babysitters? Maria glanced up at Barly who was smiling down at her. Just what was he saying?

Barly reached in his pocket for his cell, held it to his ear listening, glancing at Maria. Pocketing his cell, he pulled her into his arms. "You, okay?"

"I think so. Who called?"

"The hospital. I have to go. I'll take you back to the house."

"No, that's okay. Both our cars are here. You go to the hospital and I'll go relieve Stella and Waldo. But, Dr. B—"

"Yes, Dr. G?"

"I'll be waiting up for you."

Chapter 40

IT WAS A COMFORTABLE silence. Barly had returned home from the hospital emergency shortly after midnight. Without saying a word, they hugged—a good-to-be-home hug.

Climbing the stairs, they quietly stepped into the nursery—Maria teasing a curl around Tabby's little pink ear, Barly stroking Tommy's stray lock across his forehead. Swapping positions, Maria kissed Tommy's cheek, Barly gently tucking the blanket to Tabby's chin. Turning Maria into his arms, a quick squeeze, a quick check of the baby monitor connected to his bedroom, the doctors tiptoed down the stairs.

Barly flopped into the recliner as Maria put her hand up—he shouldn't move.

Returning with two mugs of hot chocolate topped with fluffy marshmallows, she sat in the other lounger, both content to just sit.

Sipping his cocoa, Barly smiled at a rim of marshmallow on her upper lip. "You're quite the little mother, sitting there with marshmallow—"

"What? You're telling me—" Running her tongue around her lips she tasted what was giving Barly a tickle.

"Just a couple of parents enjoying the peace and quiet after a busy day." Barly dragged an ottoman over to Maria, pulled the lever up on her lounger dropping her feet between them. "Sleepy?"

"Bone tired. You?" she asked noting the creases under his eyes.

"Same. We're going to have to give statements tomorrow. Jane and Floyd were certainly a piece of work, to say nothing of Trixie Doll and what's-his-name? Guy."

Picking up her hand, Barly paused. "So, what are we going to do with Tommy and Tabby?"

"Well, tomorrow—"

"I'm asking about the rest of their tomorrows. What are we going to do? Don't tell me their little faces, sleeping like angels, oblivious to the chaos swirling around them when we crept into their room, didn't melt your heart. I saw it on your face."

"I wasn't the only one, Dr. Bartholomew. I caught the mist in your eyes."

"Yeah? Well, Dr. Grayson, your eyes weren't exactly dry when you leaned over to kiss Tommy."

"Where are you going with this line of questioning?"

"Well, for tonight, I thought maybe ... seeing as you're here, looking so absolutely beautiful, I thought maybe we should—"

Maria leaned forward, set her empty mug on the floor and slid onto Barly's lap. "Sometimes, Dr. Bartholomew, you—"

Barly sat Maria back on the lounger and fished his ringing cell phone out of his trousers. "Hi, Mom," he said glancing at Maria. "Yes, I'm sorry I didn't call. We didn't want to wake you. Everything turned out better than we could have hoped for. The aunt *was a fake*. She was hauled off to the police station along with three others. She'll probably be charged with fraud, extortion, and some petty crimes in Raleigh."

Concern fell over Barly's face. "Maria and I are in my house ... kids are sleeping upstairs ... Mom, what's the matter? Don't cry. Everything ... of course. Drive on down in the morning. Maria and I hired a nurse to stay with the kids until we can figure out ... maybe a nanny. I'll make sure I'm home for lunch ... Maria just nodded that she'll be here too. Love you, Mom. Drive carefully."

Barly pocketed his phone, hunching his shoulders, exchanging raised brows with Maria.

"Is Chenoa all right?"

"I think so. Just emotional, wondering what happened. I should have called her on my way to the hospital. She drove back to Portland after we left the cottage. I'm sure she's tired. She mentioned she had a touch of indigestion as we left Moosehead. At any rate, we'll see tomorrow." Barly reached out for Maria's hand pulling her to her feet. "Now, Dr. Grayson, you and I are going to get some shut eye."

Snapping off the lights they walked hand in hand to his bedroom.

Hesitating, Maria wasn't quite sure what she was going to do. In the confusion, she didn't pack anything for sleeping.

Barly took care of her dilemma fishing out one of his large white T-shirts, long enough for a short nightgown. Maria changed and crawled into bed while he showered.

A towel knotted around his waist, Barly returned to the bedroom. Grinning, he turned off the bedside lamp, curling around Dr. Grayson. Her breathing was steady.

Dr. Grayson was in a deep, peaceful sleep.

Chapter 41

AT 5:32 A.M. the guardians bolted upright in Barly's mahogany sleigh bed.

Tabby, suffering urgent hunger pangs for her bottle, screeched loud and clear through the baby monitor accompanied by Tommy's sympathetic cries.

The guardians locked eyes. "I guess it's time to rise and shine, Dr. G."

"You shower, I'll get Tabby and Tommy."

"You can't carry both of them?" Barly shook his legs from the tangle of sheets.

"Right. Okay. We both go, bring them down to the kitchen. Cheerios for Tommy while I fix the bottle ... you shower ... and—" Maria's voice, shouting instructions, faded as she dashed up the stairs ... *something about cheerios.*

Barly pulling on his dark blue pajama bottoms, hopping on one foot then the other, was several steps behind.

"What time does the nurse arrive?" Maria called out. "Good morning, little girl. Oh, such big tears." Maria picked Tabby up patting her back. "What's her name ... the nurse?"

"Hildy. Come on big guy, ohhh, peww."

Maria smiled as Dr. B set about changing Tommy's very full diaper.

"Time ... Hildy—"

"6:30." Barly screwed up his face, dropping the whole smelly thing in the diaper pail.

"Good. Less than an hour and help arrives. We can do this Dr. B."

In the kitchen warming Tabby's bottle, Maria started laughing at Barly trying to get a stiffened Tommy into the highchair—baby, toddler and two adults greeting the morning in their bare feet.

Hildy arrived at 6:35. Their savior was a mid-sixties grandmother—curly gray cap of hair, rosy cheeks, with rimless glasses attached to a chain, perched on her nose. Her shoes were solid, legs and frame stocky, ready to take on any child. Thanking Hildy profusely for being so prompt, Maria smiled broadly as she handed Tabby to her with a few sucks left in her bottle.

Glancing around the kitchen, seeing everything was as in order as it was going to get, she gave Barly a hug and rushed out the back door to her car. Over her shoulder she told anyone within earshot that she was going home to shower and change, and then off to the hospital. "I'll call Stel and Waldo on the way. I'll be back for lunch."

Barly gave Hildy a brief synopsis of what had transpired at Maria's the night before.

"If Chief Roth or Detective Rodney Hall call, tell them to try our cell numbers—on the fridge. Oh, and my mother is driving down from Portland. She knows the house, has a bedroom, but don't leave her with Tommy and Tabby. She may insist but tell her I gave you strict instructions that she's supposed to rest. I'll bring you something for lunch. I'm not sure what Dr. Grayson's schedule is so I'd appreciate your staying until we get home at the end of the day. We'll have an idea when we see you at lunchtime."

"Okay, Dr. Bartholomew. Don't you worry about the little ones. I have four—all grown up, so I'm loving this."

"Thanks, Hildy. You're a Godsend."

Barly raced out the door, Jenny scooting in before the screen slammed. Turning the key in the ignition, he smiled at the man in the mirror, replaying the last hour. *Home!*

Lunch blossomed into another round of chaos. Tommy insisted that Jenny wanted to go out for a walk. Hildy assured Dr. Bartholomew that she would hold his hand and keep an eye on the dog. The trio disappeared out the back door into the yard.

Tabby didn't seem to be hungry, preferring to play bat-the-bottle out of Maria's hand, smiling with drools at the frowning big person.

Chenoa had arrived fifteen minutes before Barly and Maria rushed in the door. Sitting at the kitchen table sipping a cup of tea, she watched the melee going on around her.

Forty-five minutes later Hildy had convinced both children that naptime follows lunchtime. Chenoa disappeared into her room under her son's orders to take a nap, and that he'd be home close to five so they could talk. Hildy tucked a sandwich wrapped in wax paper into the doctors' hands shooing them out the door.

Maria whispered to Barly as they hurried to their respective cars that she thought Chenoa looked more than tired. Barly agreed. "I'll have a chat with her, check her vitals when we get home tonight."

"I have to stop at the house for more dog food and then I'll be right over," Maria said.

They paused at their cars, exchanging glances. What was happening here?

"Dr. Grayson, it might be easier if you moved in with me ... don't you think?" Barly slid into his car, winked at Maria and backed out of the driveway leaving her standing, slack jawed by the open door of her car.

Chapter 42

CHECKING ON THE LAST tiny patient, a preemie holding her own in the incubator, Maria went over the charts with the afternoon nurse, and then hurried out of the hospital to drive to Barly's house. She was worried about Chenoa and hoped that a chat, woman to woman, might shed some light on what was bothering her, why she wasn't herself.

The house was quiet when she stepped in the kitchen from the garage. Tabby was napping and Hildy offered to take Tommy and Jenny for a romp in the backyard. She said that Mrs. Bartholomew had stayed in her bedroom most of the day. Actually, she hadn't seen her at all after Barly and Maria scooted out the door at lunchtime.

Knocking softly on Chenoa's bedroom door, hearing no response, Maria opened it a crack to see if she was awake. She was startled to see her lying on the bed, pillows propping up her head, eyes open under heavy lids.

"Hi, I brought you a cup of tea. Thought you might like a little pick-me-up."

"Thank you, dear." Her voice was tired, weak, face wane. Her deep olive skin turned sallow. The light blue silky shirt fell from bony shoulders. Maria hadn't noticed before, but the woman looked frail, a loss of weight.

"You look pale. I know you had a long drive from the cottage yesterday morning, and then coming down here, but it seems more than that. What—"

"Sit, dear." Chenoa patted the bed. "I don't know what to do. You must promise me you won't tell Barly." Pain filled her eyes, brows knit together, seeking Maria's agreement.

"What is it, Chenoa?"

"If I do nothing … my doctor—" She waved her hand dismissively, letting it drop to the quilt. "My doctor said I have a blockage … my heart. It's bad. If Barly finds out, and something happens to me, he'll blame himself. I know he will—his father, Julie—yet I want his advice … no. I can't ask him. If it's my time … then it's God's will."

"Chenoa, you have to tell him. I know he's worried about you. You're pale … weak. Talk to him. He'll be home soon. He can help."

"No, no. You said you wouldn't tell him."

"I have to tell him … but it would be better if you did. Please, say you will. You have to trust him."

Chenoa lifted her head, alarm written in her large black eyes. Her head shook slightly, then fell back on the pillow as Maria picked up the artist's hand, holding it to her cheek.

Chapter 43

SIPPING A CUP OF TEA, Maria watched Jenny drop a ball in Tommy's lap. Giggles erupted as he threw the ball, mimicking Hildy. The ball landed a few inches from his feet. He thought his toss was wonderful, clapping as Jenny snatched it and ran around the yard, then dropped the slobbery yellow thing in the little boy's lap, falling between his outstretched hands.

Maria watched the game of fetch but her mind was with Chenoa. What if she didn't tell her son? It would devastate Barly if something happened. He once again would blame himself. Maria decided she'd give Chenoa a chance to tell him, but if she didn't by dinner time, then she would. There is nothing worse than a patient who hides pain and symptoms from her doctor, in this case her own son. Smiling through her worry lines, Maria retrieved her cell. Chief Roth's name appeared on the display.

"Hello, Chief. How are the Flintrock sisters behaving?"

"After giving the Raleigh PD Chief my report, he dispatched a van to pick up Jane and Trixie—should arrive tomorrow. Detective Hall may have to go down—give his side of the story. Dr. Grayson, I'm calling about another matter that you asked me to look into."

"My adopting Tabby and Tommy?"

"Yes. I had an extensive meeting with Children's Services. As you know, they were holding off picking up the children until after the grandparents arrived which is now a few weeks ago."

"I asked them for more time."

"Well, on an exploratory basis, like you asked, they can't see their way to giving a thumbs up on the idea of your adopting the children. Their recommendation, one way or the other, carries a lot of weight. In fact, the court rarely rules against their recommendation."

Maria closed her eyes, Tommy's image playing ball with Jenny lingering in her mind.

"Dr. Grayson, you still there?"

Maria drew in a deep breath. "Yes, Chief. I'm here. What reasons did Children's Services give?"

"Basically, your life over the past few years clouded the prospect, issues with killing two men—"

"In self defense!"

"I know, I know … the death of your husband. You'd be a single mom, no roots moving three times from one state to another and back … well, bottom line, they will not recommend an adoption take place under the present circumstances. They are against your adopting the pair. They were quick to add that they thought given some time, their recommendation might be different. Just not now, not with these two children."

"I see. Thanks for looking into it for me." Maria looked away, out the window, blinking rapidly.

"I'm sorry," Roth said.

"Me, too."

Slowly folding her cell, Maria looked at Hildy carrying Tabby on her hip, testing the nippled bottle of milk on her wrist. "Thanks, Hildy. I'll feed her. You go back out with Tommy."

A tear splashed from Maria's eye onto the baby's cheek. She quickly steeled herself not to allow any more tears to form. "Here, baby girl, nice warm milk for your tummy. That's a precious little one." Maria smiled as Tabby vigorously sucked on the bottle, her little legs kicking with glee.

Hearing Barly's Jeep pull into the driveway, Maria kissed the baby's cheek, cradling her with her bottle. She mustn't let on what Roth just told her, and she would not tell Barly tonight. She would not add to his worries. He will have burdens way beyond mine this evening, she thought. Rocking Tabby, she looked to the ceiling and prayed. *God, God, God, hold Chenoa. Hold Barly. Please, please, please hold them safe. I love them. They are such good people. God … hold them safe.*

Hearing Barly's footsteps as he entered the kitchen, Maria drew her lips up in a smile to greet him.

Chapter 44

———

BARLY SWUNG THROUGH THE door setting his black doctor's bag on the kitchen table. He had rushed straight home from his practice. He was dressed in his usual office uniform—black pants, white short-sleeved shirt open at the neck—his version of a doctor's casual attire to present professional confidence without instilling the white coat syndrome—fear. He especially wanted the casual approach for his mom.

"Well, this is a pretty sight—my two girls sitting pretty as a picture." He kissed Tabby's pink cheek, her blue eyes following him without a pause on the sucking sound. He turned to Maria giving her a peck on the cheek, noting her eyes seeking his. He saw trouble there.

She looked up at him. "Did you see Tommy on your way in?"

"I did. He sure has walking down, but the running … not so good. His body moves faster than his feet. He doesn't care, just laughs, tugging on Jenny to help him up. They're quite a pair. I'll check on Mom and then we'll talk."

Maria nodded, switching Tabby to her shoulder. She was immediately rewarded with a loud burp followed by the hiccups. Barly smiled, checking Maria's eyes once more. Yup, something was wrong. Picking up his bag, he strode to his mother's room, knocked, and let himself in.

Chenoa had gathered her strength moving from her bed to a wingback chair next to the window. Her eyes followed her son setting the black bag on the bed, her husband's bag that Barly always kept close by. Smiling at his mother sitting stoically straight in the chair, he pulled up a stool in front of her, taking hold of her hands folded in her lap.

"Okay, young lady, no stalling. Tell me what's wrong." He turned her palm up, his fingers on her wrist. Her pulse was weak. "Do I have to pry it out of you?"

Of course, he knew what was wrong. He had called her doctor in Portland as soon as he entered the office this morning.

The doctor was forthcoming. "Your mother was in for an electrocardiogram and a stress test two months ago. She had significant coronary artery blockage at that time and I wanted to admit her for further tests. She deferred, told me she would follow up with you."

"She didn't."

"I'll send her records to you right away."

"Thanks, send everything you have. Hang on, my nurse will come on the line, give you the email address here at my practice."

That conversation was several hours ago. Since that time Barly had received and poured over his mother's test results and was in immediate communication with Dr. Farrell, a heart surgeon affiliated with White Pines Memorial. He was on a fishing trip but was cutting it short. He figured he would be back at the hospital by ten tonight. "Leave your mother's test results with my surgical team's head nurse. I'll be ready to take over Mrs. Bartholomew's case unless we concur that she could return to Portland."

Barly folded his mother's hands in his, raising his eyes to hers, wanting her to confide in him, to trust him.

"My heart ... it's giving out." Chenoa's eyes filled with tears, she turned away hoping he wouldn't see. "I'm afraid ... for you."

"You saw your doctor?"

"Yes."

"What did he say?"

"A blockage."

"Mom, look at me." Barly lifted her chin turning her tear-stained face to him. "We can fix this. Don't be afraid."

"Barly, no—" Grimacing, a veil of pain covered her face.

"Stay where you are, Mom. Don't go back to bed. I'm calling the Medi-Van."

"No." She gasped, shaking her head, her hand fumbling for his.

Barly's voice was soft, reassuring. "Some tests are needed. We have to know exactly what we're dealing with. That's all. A few tests that are best administered at the hospital."

"You're forgetting I was married to a doctor ... I know what you're saying."

"That's right, and you also know that doctors have to have test results in order to treat the patient. Promise me you'll stay in the chair?"

Dropping his hand she nodded that she understood.

Barly leaned over kissing her forehead and walked out of bedroom closing the door softly behind him.

Hurrying to the kitchen, cell to his ear, he placed a call to the hospital. "Hello, this is Dr. Bartholomew. Please dispatch an ambulance to my house, stat. Seventy-two-year-old woman, coronary artery blockage. She is to be transported on a stretcher. Do not, I repeat, do not let her get to her feet. She's to be taken to the ER. Assemble the cardiac surgery team. I want a full lab workup on the woman's heart, all vitals."

"The patient's name?"

"Chenoa Bartholomew. My mother."

Chapter 45

———

THE SCENE IN THE kitchen was surreal—copper pots hanging on the rack over the island glistening in the late afternoon sunlight.

Maria stood holding Tabby sucking on her pacifier, the only sound. She saw the worry written on Barly's face as he stepped to her, folding her and the baby in a quick hug.

"It's bad?" She looked up at him hoping it wasn't, knowing it was.

"Yeah. The ambulance will be here in a few minutes. Can you call Stella? Ask if she and Waldo can help you take the children back to your house ... with all their stuff."

The screen door banged open and a whoosh of a little boy with a dog raced in. Tommy giggled as he fell against Barly, circling his arms around his pant leg for support.

"I heard," Hildy said latching the screen. "I can go with you, Dr. Grayson. Stay with Tommy and help in case you want to go to the hospital."

"Thank you, Hildy." Maria's eyes never left Barly's, unspoken words bouncing to each other, back and forth, silent words that Chenoa was in a battle for her life. "Who will operate?"

"Farrell."

"When?"

"Depends on the test results. Farrell's fishing. Cutting his trip short. He said he should be back about ten tonight. We'll wait until morning ... if we can." Barly swept a loose strand of auburn hair behind her ear, his touch tender.

She laid her fingers over his—*I'm here with you.* "She couldn't have a better team of doctors. She'll pull through. She's tough, Barly. Call me when you schedule the operation?"

"I will—"

Both looked out the window at the sound.

As instructed, the medics backed into the driveway, no siren. Two medics jumped out, pulled a gurney from the back releasing the wheels and hotfooted it to the screen door Hildy had unlatched and was holding open.

Barly nodded to the two husky men in black jumpsuits to follow him. Maria handed Tabby to Hildy and followed the men.

Chenoa didn't fuss. She knew the drill preparing herself for what was to come. Her son was in charge, but fear filled her face, not for her but for him.

"Okay, Mom. Up you go."

On the count of three the two medics and two doctors transferred Chenoa from the chair to a prone position on the gurney. Maria and Barly exchanged a swift glance—she was light as a feather. Her loose clothing had camouflaged her weight loss.

A medic stepped to each end of the gurney which they wheeled over the floor, then carried down two steps to the van.

Chenoa's eyes wide, seeking Barly—her hand moved sharply to her chest.

"I'm here, Mom. See you in a few minutes. Draw a little blood, take some tests and then I'll give you something for the discomfort. Okay?"

Chenoa nodded. Closing her eyes, brows scrunched.

Maria bent, kissed her check. "Chenoa, I'll see you later. After your tests. You couldn't be in better hands. You'll be okay." She stepped back as the medics eased the gurney into the ambulance.

Turning to Barly, putting her hands on his cheeks, a quick kiss on his lips, a hug. "I'll see you at the hospital as soon as the kids are moved. You're the best, sweetheart."

Her fingers ran down his bare arms, releasing him. Please, please, dear God, do you hear me? Give them strength.

The ambulance backed out of the driveway, followed by the Jeep.

Chapter 46

SCANNING THE BATTERY OF tests, Barly knew what had to be done, and it had to be done quickly before it was too late. He called Dr. Farrell apprising him of the situation. Neither man said the words: Bartholomew, Chenoa, or mother.

Bypass surgery, both doctors agreed, had to be performed as soon as possible requiring veins from her legs. Two arteries were almost totally blocked.

Even though Barly knew what had to be done, Farrell went over the list so there was no misunderstanding while he was driving from Vermont to Maine: match the blood type, set aside several pints. Also, instruct the team to begin prepping the patient. Tell the anesthesiologist to be ready, but not to start the drip until Farrell walked through the door, hands scrubbed, ready for latex gloves, ready to be swathed head to foot in a surgical gown, cap, mask, and headband with lamp and magnifying glass.

Barly added an instruction: the patient's face was to be shielded.

Dr. Bartholomew was also prepped. He would be ready to assist.

THE TEAM IN BLUE surgical gowns and caps, white masks in place, glanced at the clock.

Fifteen minutes after ten. All tests were complete, the patient sedated ready to be put under.

The door between the scrub room and the operating theater swung open. A nurse signaled to Barly to step out of the OR—she had a message.

"Dr. Farrell has been in an accident. He's been transported to a hospital in Manchester, New Hampshire. His injuries are not life threatening ... but he won't be operating. I called Portland. The cardio surgeon is up in Bangor. He's arranging transportation. He's on his way."

"How long?" Barly's stared at the young nurse, waiting for her answer.

"Four hours minimum, maybe longer. He's trying to get a charter, but with the July Fourth holiday ...

"Dr. Bartholomew," the cardio head nurse broke through the door. "The patient ... she's going into cardiac arrest." The nurse stood at the door to the OR, holding it open, waiting for the surgeon.

Barly drew in a long breath. "Tell the Portland hospital that the double bypass surgery has begun and that the surgeon should get here as fast as he can. Call in our resident surgeon, Dr. Thomas to assist. Stat."

The young nurse, calm, in control, said, "He's in surgery, Doctor. I'll check to see how long—"

"Tell him I need him. Let another doctor close and he's to join me as soon as he is able."

Scrubbed fists in the air, Barly turned on his heel, reentering the chilled, brilliant white OR. The only visible sign of concern—blood pumping at his temples. He had performed this surgery many times. It was his specialty, all successful but for one—Julie. There was no reason this by-pass surgery should fail except that it was his mother. She was dying. He could not wait.

He checked that the lowering of the body temperature was complete—placing the patient in a hypothermic state, reducing the brain and other tissues' demand for oxygen. Nodding to the anesthesiologist and the nurse monitoring the patient's vitals, he visualized the initial steps of the procedure. Glancing at the clock, Barly began the surgery.

Many times he had lectured interns and residents alike that bypass surgery was really a fancy, sophisticated plumbing procedure. You make an incision in the breastbone, saw through that breastbone, opening it as you would a three-ring binder, and later rewire it together. Bypass with what? Blood vessels harvested from the leg—a vein. The whole procedure taking three to four hours—prep time, opening the patient's breastbone, harvesting the veins from the legs, and then ensuring that everything is closed properly. With training, and experience, the success rate of the procedure is very high ... even if an emergency and the patient is your mother.

Right?

Dr. Bartholomew made the initial incision—the operation had begun.

Chapter 47

————

AFTER GRAFTING THE LEG veins during the "on pump" procedure, the heart-lung machine was turned off. Chenoa's heart started beating on its own, the blood flow returning to normal.

The patient was alive—at least she was still clinging to life.

The operation was complete.

Barly thanked the team, praising their work, and left the brilliant white OR.

Stripping off the bloodied surgical gown, gloves, and cap, his fingers gripped the edge of the sink. He felt Maria enter the small scrub room, felt her comforting arms, her head resting on his shoulder blade.

"She made it, Barly."

"We don't know yet. The next few hours are critical."

"I know … her heart?"

"My God, Maria, I held her heart in my hands," he whispered.

Maria felt a tear on her fingers, her hold tightened around him. "As she gave you life, today you gave her life. You were masterful in there. I've never seen anything like it. The team performed with precision, everything you asked of them."

"Yes, they did. Everything."

"I love you."

He had waited for her to say those words, knowing he had to wait until she was ready, never daring to ask her.

He slowly turned his back to the scrub sink, two tear-stained faces sought each other's eyes understanding the magnitude of the words, understanding the magnitude of the surgery he had just performed. Gathering her in his arms, he held on, she held on, together … holding each other.

"I love you too, Maria. You'll never know how much."

The kiss was warm, tender.

Caressing her hair, he tucked her head under his chin.

"Over five hours … you're exhausted." Lifting her head, she wiped the tears from his eyes. "Go freshen up. I'll wait for you in the ICU. I'll sit with Chenoa."

"Maria, this afternoon, or yesterday I guess, I saw something on your face but attributed it to concern over my mom. Tell me what it was."

No walls went up, she was with the man she cherished more than life itself, he had breached the barriers and she would no longer hide. "Chief Roth called. It seems I'm not fit to be a mom … not now anyway … maybe in the future. Children's Services, given everything I've been involved in over the last three years, will block my adopting Tabby and Tommy."

Holding her head to his chest, he sighed. "Shortsighted. We'll just see about that—"

Maria held a finger to his lips. "No bad thoughts. Not now. Time for that later. Let's go see your mom. She needs us."

Chapter 48

———

IT WAS AFTER FOUR in the morning, when Barly entered the ICU. Maria had changed into a fresh, white cotton dress, a green blanket was draped over her knees. She was sitting at his mother's bedside holding the woman's vein-lined hand in her delicate fingers, her head resting on the bedcovers in a light sleep. He quietly pulled up a chair to the other side of the bed.

The dim light of the monitors, sending shadows on the pale yellow walls, displayed Chenoa's electrocardiogram tracing, blood pressure, breathing rate and oxygen level. A trachea tube inserted during her surgery assisted her breathing with a ventilator. A monitor also displayed each beat of her heart, regulated by a temporary pacemaker Barly had positioned in her chest until her condition improved, and beyond if warranted. Tubes to drain fluid were positioned in her chest before he rewired the breastbone together. A special IV drip helped with her blood pressure, and to control any problems with bleeding.

Chenoa looked small, frail, lying in the bed with wires, tubes, and ticking monitors. She would remain heavily sedated for several hours.

Feeling a slight pressure on her fingers, Maria lifted her head in time to see Chenoa's eyelids flutter. Maria squeezed her hand, picked up a chip of ice from the dish on the bed stand and traced Chenoa's parched lips. Her violet eyes shifted to Barly as he gently pressed his lips to the top of his mother's hand careful not to touch the needle inserted under the thin weathered skin. Chenoa blinked and then fell back to sleep.

Exchanging glances, Maria laid her head down again on the bed. Barly walked to her, leaned over her, hands on either side against

TWISTS OF FATE | 171

the blanket and kissed the top of her head then moved to a more comfortable chair. Unbuttoning the top two buttons on his white shirt, he laid his head back. His black trousers hitched up showing a few inches of his black and white diamond argyle socks—a hint of humor hidden by the otherwise serious cardio doctor. Both relaxed into a light sleep.

A few hours later the sky turned gray, then gradually filled the room with sunlight. Maria, shivering slightly in the cold temperature of the room, reached for her cell vibrating in the pocket of her black cardigan sweater.

"Hi, Stel," she whispered stepping to the doorway.

"Hey, good morning. Is it over? How'd it go?"

Maria glanced back at Barly, his eyes open at the sound of her voice. "She made it, thanks to the incredible Dr. Bartholomew. How are the Double Ts?"

"Well … actually … that's why I'm calling."

"What's wrong, Stel?"

Maria's eyes darted, fixed on Barly as he snapped upright with the tension building in her low whisper.

"The Caldwells just phoned. They'll be here day after tomorrow, around noon. Mr. Caldwell said he has a signed court order giving them custody of Tabatha *and* Tommy." They're coming to take the children back to North Carolina."

Chapter 49

———

VERIFICATION!

The temporary guardians were not going to hand over the children they saved without verification.

Tapping the number, Maria held her cell to her ear, her left hand holding her arm steady.

"Hey, girlfriend. Manny just this minute asked me if I heard how the operation went."

"Five hours, Liz. Barly handled the whole thing."

"How? I thought docs weren't supposed to operate on a family member."

"They aren't supposed to ... unless it's an emergency. The scheduled surgeon was in a car accident in New Hampshire."

"Holy cow. How's Barly's mom doing?"

"We're in her room now. She's sleeping. Liz, I hate to ask you, but we need your help again."

"Wait, let me put you on speaker. Manny's eating his breakfast—Cheerios. Go figure."

"Hi, Maria. Liz did a thumbs up on Barly's mom. What can we do for you?" Manny asked, his voice muffled but understandable.

"Stella just called. The Caldwells are coming for the kids, both of them. They told Stella that they have papers giving them custody—a signed court order. Do you have a way of verifying this?"

"Easy Peasy. Text us the grandparent's names, first and last, address, phone number. This is just to verify that what we already have is correct. We'll be back in a couple of hours, or less. At least we'll have an update."

"They told Stella they'd be here by noon, day after tomorrow."

"Hang tight. Bye for now." Liz rang off.

Maria pocketed her cell as Barly took her in his arms. "What are we going to do?" Her voice a whisper into his shirt.

"I doubt the Caldwells would lie. Plain and simple, they had a change of heart. We'll know soon enough. Why don't you go home, check on things. Call Hildy, or Harriett, and take a nap if you can."

"I don't want to leave Chenoa, and you're the one who needs a nap."

"We both know she's going to be out of it for a few hours. I'll check in with my practice and come right back. I want to be here when Mom wakes up. I'll rest while I wait."

"Okay. I'll meet you back here—less than two hours. Call me if there's a change."

"I will."

"Promise?"

"I promise." Lifting her chin, he looked into her eyes. "Did you mean what you said in the scrub room?"

"Yes. You?"

Kissing her plump lips once more, he leaned away. "Yes, I love you."

———

ROCKING TABBY, THE BABY sucking furiously on her bottle, Maria gazed into her big blue eyes. "You're going to drive the boys crazy with those baby blues, you know that don't you? Yes, I'm talking to you."

Maria picked up her cell on the lamp table. It was Liz. Inhaling a deep breath, she pressed the green button.

"Hi. What did you find out?"

"It's legit. Not only that, crazy Trixie Doll has visitation rights ... in writing. I spoke with the Caldwell's lawyer, who emailed me a copy of the court order stating that the Caldwells were assigned as guardians for Tabatha and Tommy, father Stephen Caldwell deceased ... yada yada."

"Barly thought as much. He didn't think the grandfather would lie. Did their lawyer say anything about their plans?"

"Yup. Just as they told Stella—arrive in York by noon, day after tomorrow. The one piece of new info I learned is that two neighbors, house on the left, house on the right, are listed as guardians in the event something happens to the Caldwells. And, girlfriend, they have a mini bus of some kind. They're all coming to York. So, if it's okay with you, Manny and I are flying up tomorrow afternoon. Moral support type of thing. Make sure nobody pulls a fast one. Is that okay?"

"Absolutely. Drop your stuff in your room at my house. Stella … or somebody at the house will know where we are—either the house or the hospital. Call me after Tommy lets go of Manny. You know how he likes the men. Take an early flight—tomorrow is the fourth. Must be fireworks somewhere. Tommy would love it." Maria closed her cell wiping an errant tear from her cheek.

Chapter 50

———

TABBY WAS CRYING ... faraway ... or was she dreaming?

Rubbing her eyes, Maria rolled over to sit on the edge of the bed. Sleep wasn't in the cards. There was too much to do. Glancing at the clock, she was surprised to see she had slept for three hours. The events over the last twenty-four or so hours suddenly hit her in the stomach. Chenoa, Stella's call, conversations with Liz ... the grandparents were on their way to take custody of the little ones.

Emotions coursed through her body. The scrub room. She told Barly she loved him. He said he loved her. Closing her eyes, she felt his arms around her, heard the words he whispered in her ear—*I love you.*

Knowing the children were leaving hung heavy on their hearts. They were both hurting.

Her eyes popped open wide. The children! This was their last day with them. Their clothes, toys, everything had to be packed ... no more drooling baby with big blue eyes. No more slurppy ball dropped in Tommy's lap from his furry playmate. No more Tommy lifting his little arms to Barly. They were going to a new place with their grandparents, maybe even spend time with their crazy-haired mother.

This was how it should be—home surrounded by a big loving family made up of neighbors, friends who will nurture them, making sure they grow up surrounded by people who love them.

Better than two doctors, darting from one emergency to another. But ... what does that say about Barly and me? Does it mean there are no children in our future?

Come on, Maria. That's nonsense. Other doctors do it ... have families. You're getting ahead of yourself. But hold on—just because

Barly said he loves you … and you love him … doesn't mean he wants to marry you. He may back away … no, he thought I should move in with him. Of course, he could have been joking…

"Hey up there."

Bursting through the door, Liz came to a standstill staring at Maria. She was followed by Manny both dressed as usual—black shirt to black shoes.

"Oh no, girlfriend. No sad face. Where's that camera of yours. I see it. One pic of mournful you. Tomorrow I want a happy face. Great. Got it. Now give us our duties. We didn't fly up to hold your hand. There's work to do."

Manny stood behind his wife, grinning, hand on her shoulder. He loved to see her in action, her red ringlets sparking. "We met the drill sergeant in the kitchen. I think she said her name was Sergeant Hildy."

Laughing, Maria hugged Liz, then Manny. "OK. First call the grandparents. Do they need baby furniture? Then start packing up the nursery. Everything except what they'll need for the trip to North Carolina. Hildy will know. There are boxes in the basement from my move. I have to run to the hospital, see Chenoa. Be back in an hour." She looked at Manny and back to Liz. "You two are better than winning the lottery."

"Well, I don't think that's quite—" Liz was wagging her head.

"We'll take it. Now on your way. Come on Stitch, let's make the call to the GPs."

Liz hugged her husband. She loved it when he called her Stitch.

"Let Hildy know what you're doing so she won't worry. She'll take care of the double Ts," Maria called over her shoulder as she skipped down the stairs, a quick stop in the kitchen kissing baby drool and accepting a cheerio from Tommy's gooey fingers.

———

TIPTOEING INTO CHENOA'S room in the ICU, Maria was pleasantly surprised at how she looked. The trachea had been removed and a little color had returned to her cheeks. The monitors continued to record her body's vitals. Scanning the displays, Maria could see that not only did she look better but her system was responding to the increased blood flow through the veins Barly had grafted to her heart. Maria gently picked up her hand, kissed her fingers. Feeling the kiss, Chenoa opened her eyes, a smile on her lips.

"You're doing so well. Is the pain tolerable?" Maria said in her soft velvety voice.

"Yes, dear." Chenoa mouthed the words. Her voice faint but a smile spread across her face.

How wonderful to hear her speak even if only a whisper. It was a strong whisper overcoming the discomfort the trachea caused in her throat.

"From the looks of the tracings, the monitors ... the nurses will be unhooking you soon. You'll be up for a few minutes in a chair tomorrow. I'm sure of it. Don't talk. I know it hurts. So much has happened. Let me fill you in and then I'll let you sleep."

Maria talked so fast that Chenoa shook her head ever so slightly delighting in her enthusiasm, noting the gleam in the doctor's eyes that had been missing.

Feeling the vibration of her cell, seeing it was Liz, Maria put her on speaker so Chenoa could hear the latest.

Liz began her report before Maria could tell her Chenoa was listening. "We talked to the GPs. They're on the road, Inter 95."

Maria mouthed to Chenoa that GP meant grandparents.

"They didn't need the furniture. Had set up a room. But then they called back—not two minutes later. They want it all—stuff from your house and Barly's. Honest to God, girlfriend, they're acting like a couple of school kids. They're all traveling together— GPs and their neighbors in a van. So I guess they discussed it and decided they could use everything you had. Going to set up nurseries around the neighborhood, ready for baby-sitting duties."

"Sounds wonderful, Liz—"

"Wait, wait. Manny just finished with another call from the GPs ... they're stressed out ... don't know how they can get the furniture back to NC in time ... Manny says we're going to rent a U-Hauler. But the GPs don't know how to hook it up. I told Manny to tell the GPs, easy peasy, we'll do it. That's it. We're on our way to Barly's to get the cribbies. Back to your house. Be ready to transfer the stuff from your nursery to the hauler after the kiddies get up. Manny and I are thinking about having kids. Says he's waiting to see how the fireworks go tonight. Bye."

Maria and Chenoa smiled at each other through happy tears after hearing Liz's report. "I think I'd better go check on my patients. I'll stop back before going home. Barly and I will be having dinner with you. Fill you in on the latest before the fireworks." Kissing Chenoa's forehead, Maria hustled out of the ICU, saying a prayer of thanks for Liz and Manny.

Passing Barly on his way to the ICU, exchanging a quick hug, she rattled off a brief synopsis about the grandparents and told him that she would join him for a pudding dinner with Chenoa, then on to the Fourth celebration.

Liz called again. "Waldo and Stella met us at Barly's to help. They had the zoo-van. Honestly, Maria, I'm glad we had the U-Hauler. Zoo-van was transporting a verrry long sicko snake. Give me a gator any day. Anyway, Hildy made a list of stuff—diapers, formula, cheerios. Then she called back and doubled the order."

"Oh my God, we are going to owe you big time," Maria said chuckling.

"Girlfriend, you have no idea. We thought maybe a weekend at the cottage, then a week. Manny said he's upping it to a month. Maybe we can timeshare. We are definitely rethinking the kid thing. We can't believe how much stuff you have to have for two little people."

———

AFTER THEIR PUDDING DINNER with Chenoa, Barly and Maria raced to her house to rendezvous with Liz and Manny, and Stella and Waldo. Stella had bundled up Tabby, and was having a very serious conversation on why Tommy should wear a sweater in the cool night air, and, no, Jenny couldn't come to the fireworks. The boom booms would scare the dog.

Waldo opened the back of the zoo-van, as Liz dubbed it, so they could pack what they needed to sit on the grass overlooking the barge by Ellis Park Sand Beach to see the fireworks.

Liz, hands on her hips, kept saying she thought they packed everything, where did all this come from, it's just a few fireworks. Waldo explained that he and Stella unpacked the back of the U-hauler, stashing the stuff in the zoo-van: two strollers, a playpen just in case Tommy started to wander, then a six-pack of beer for the men, wine for the ladies, a milk and a water bottle for Tabby, and Apple juice in a sippy cup for Tommy, and, God Almighty, they almost forgot the cheerios.

At the beach Waldo and Manny found a perfect spot which required unloading the zoo-van.

Oohs and ahhs followed along with drinks and cheerios. In the confusion of unpacking and packing they forgot the picnic basket Hildy had put together with chips, dips, nuts and cookies.

After the final boom booms and the big ta-da, everything was packed back in the zoo-van.

Maria overheard Manny tell Liz he was going to talk to Barly about getting snipped.

Chapter 51

———

A LIGHT BLUE VAN pulled up, horn honking, turning into Maria's driveway and parked behind the white zoo-van. The blue van was painted with a name on each side in foot-high letters: *Tommy* in red, *Tabatha* in white.

Sylvia and Steven Caldwell climbed out, Steven helping his wife navigate the step. The driver and a pair of neighbors followed. The wife of the driver opened the windows freeing orange, yellow, pink and blue balloons, tied with ribbons on the inside door handles. So much helium Liz thought they were lucky the weight of the van tethered the vehicle to the ground. A CD, volume on high, played the music of an ice cream truck at full tilt, programmed to keep repeating.

"Now that's how you make an entrance," Liz said clapping her hands, hustling up to the Caldwells, Manny by her side, hugging the Caldwells, then the neighbors.

Maria and Barly, holding hands, stepped out the front door, eyes wide in amusement, joining the melee of hugs, introductions, and joyful tears. Maria squeezed Barly's hand, then pulled her red camera from her capris pocket and began snapping, which sent the neighbors into comedy mode—crazy faces, crossed eyes, and hand gestures with fingers as rabbit ears over the heads of the person standing next to them.

Hildy came to the front door holding Tabby. Tommy clung to her apron until he saw Jenny dashing about the new big people. Squealing, he turned, easing down the steps to join the fun. Stumbling on the grass, falling to his knees, giggling, he reached for a fist of Jenny's fur to pull him up--*unsuccessfully*.

"There, there, Tommy. What a brave boy you are. No tears." Squatting in front of the toddler, Mr. Caldwell lifted him, steadying him on his chubby legs.

Maria and Barly exchanged glances. This was quite a change from the last visit. They had chatted with Tommy, preparing him that his Grampy would be coming shortly. They wondered what he would do next, but Tommy was ahead of them. A grin spread from ear to ear. "Grampy?"

"Yes, Grampy. Grammy and Grampy want you and Tabby to come live with us."

"Jenny?"

"Umm, I don't think ..."

His thought was cut short when Stella and Waldo joined the group. The bedlam started all over again when the Caldwells and the neighbors learned the zoo-van was his. The bedlam turned rowdy with slaps on Doc Whistle's back as Stella flashed the diamond on her finger.

"How do you like these sparklers, Maria?"

"Beyond liking. I'm so happy for you, Stella. I want all the details ... soon." Maria kept snapping pictures she would share with Chenoa tonight.

Tabby began screaming. She didn't care what was going on, she wanted her noon bottle. Hildy carried her away from the pandemonium, cooing to her that she understood, and she'd have her bottle forthwith.

"How about we all sit a minute. Lemonade on the back patio?" Maria said.

"Sounds like a plan, girlfriend." Liz looped her arm through Mrs. Caldwell's. "Let's lead this parade, shall we?"

Manny dropped back to Mr. Caldwell, who had paused watching Tommy and Jenny. "I suppose the doctors want to see the court order."

"Oh, I don't think that will be necessary. They asked Liz and I to check, I hope you don't mind. I told them everything was in order. Today is difficult for them. They've become attached to the kids— but, they recognize that family trumps them. They've accepted it."

"Hell of a thing, that orphanage selling Tabatha. The wife and I were sick when we heard."

"Mr. Caldwell, things have a way of righting themselves. The FBI set up a sting on the Sinclairs, the owners of the orphanage. Mrs. Thompson, the woman who called the tip line here in York, and who thought she was adopting a baby girl, helped the agents set up the sting—recording conversations with the Sinclairs to be used as evidence of their nefarious acts in baby trafficking."

"She's a brave woman. Sylvia and I felt sorry for her. Terrible. Terrible."

"You'll be glad to hear that Mrs. Thompson, after testifying, turned right around and set up an organization to solicit donations to help stop the selling of babies. Her $190,000 was returned and she donated it all to her new organization. I'm sure she would be more than glad to hear from you and how Tabatha is doing."

"We'll do it. Anything to help." Mr. Caldwell shook his head. "Then Trisandra showing up. When Dr. Bartholomew called with that piece of news, Sylvia said to me, right then and there, that we had to step up for our Stevie's sake. But we didn't see how we could manage. Our neighbors were with us when you called. They discussed the situation and came up with a plan, said they'd help. And as you can see, they are helping BIG time."

Mr. Caldwell, nodding to his wife, took Tommy's hand, led him around the house to the side of the blue van, waving at Barly for help. The neighbors, smiling at each other conspiratorially, followed, as did the others wondering what was up.

Jenny began dashing around the yard, but hearing a soft bark darted to Tommy's side. Mr. Caldwell opened the back of the van and, grinning at Barly, together they set a crate on the ground and opened the door. A Golden Retriever puppy darted out, slurping Tommy's gleeful face, running under Jenny's tummy, rolling on the ground. Tommy, giggling, fell on the grass beside her.

Waldo then put two fingers to his lips, and whistled for attention. "Anybody ready to help hook up this U-Hauler to that blue bus?"

Three male chests puffed out, wives of the neighbor men felt their husbands' muscles, announcing they were qualified to handle the task. The driver neighbor became second in command, conferring with Waldo on how best to accomplish the mission at hand. The two determined the location of the van was just right except there was no room to maneuver the U-Haul onto the hitch for towing. The driver pulled out into the street, backing up to the tongue of the U-Haul. The men, having been proclaimed fit for the task, lifted the U-Haul tongue onto the hitch mounted on the back of the van, all the while groaning, moaning at how heavy it was.

Maria kept the little red camera set to video, capturing the scene with sound.

Liz stood next to her. "See, girlfriend. I told you, easy peasy."

Barly, Manny, and Waldo had loaded the nursery furniture in the U-Haul, along with all the boxes of diapers, formula, toys, paraphernalia taken to the fireworks, and a wardrobe of clothes fit for a little prince and princess to travel in style.

Jenny rolled on the grass, letting the puppy and Tommy crawl over her, then, barking, raced away. The puppy in a hurry to follow kept falling. Tommy not to be out done toddled after them giggling every time Jenny ran up to him, slurping his little face with her best kiss.

Suddenly it was over.

Hugs, kisses, tears were exchanged. Maria kissed Tabby goodbye, as she strapped the sleeping baby in her new car seat. Barly kissed and hugged Tommy then strapped him in his new car seat. Grampy sat on one side, the crate holding a puppy named Jenny in the aisle next to him.

Stella wiped a tear from her eye as she waved to the blue van, Doc Whistle's arm around her waist.

Maria snapped pictures through her tears, Barly's arm around her shoulders as they walked down the driveway, waving at the blue van turning the corner. Maria sucked in a big gulp of air, batting her lashes to stop the tears. Barly's arm tightened, his lashes flicking in unison with Maria's.

"Well, girlfriend, Manny and I are heading to Boston. We have a flight to Orlando in a few hours. You okay?"

Maria nodded, folding her friend in her arms. "Thank you for everything." Then hugged Manny, thanking him.

Barly and Manny shared a manly hug.

Liz punched Barly's bicep. "Now, don't forget … the timeshare junket. I hear it's nice at the lake in the winter—snowmobiling, making love by the fire." Seeing the startled expression on Barly's face she laughed pulling him into a hug.

"Call, text … let me know you're home safe." Maria took one more picture of Manny giving Liz a peck on the cheek, then handed the camera to Manny to take a picture of the two girlfriends, giggling, something about maybe a kid thing wouldn't be so bad.

Barly squatted on the grass scratching Jenny's ears as they watched the last vehicle in the line, Doc Whistle's Pet Clinic, Nails to Tails, disappear around the corner.

They had released the children to their new guardians. It had taken less than an hour. And now there was silence.

Silence.

A Black-Capped Chickadee, singing its sweet song, broke through the silence, a song that all was right in their world.

Maria looked up at the old maple tree. "Jenny's going to miss the activity. That puppy was cute."

Barly grasped Maria's hand. "Old man Caldwell is a smart cookie. Tommy never realized his life changed that minute. Slick. Very slick."

Barly stood, hugged her close. "What say we go to the Stage Neck Inn for dinner? I don't know about you, but I'd like to decompress after the last few weeks."

"Sounds wonderful. Then see Chenoa?"

"Yup. I'll run home, freshen up. Pick you up in two hours? Give you time for a nap."

"I'll be ready."

She watched his Jeep turn the corner, and with a sigh looked down at Jenny. "Just you and me again, girl. The kids, a puppy … gone. You're going to need therapy."

Jenny looked up at a seagull squawking, riding the wind, and then trotted into the house flopping on her doggie bed in the living room.

Chapter 52

——

DÉJÀ VU!

His eyes were on the road but his hand covered hers resting on the leather seat of his black Mercedes. He felt good. No, he felt great, smiling as he turned down the hill to the inn. It was a beautiful evening. He had planned a walk on the beach after dinner.

The maître d' smiled as one of his favorite people walked in, the handsome man with salt and pepper hair impeccably dressed in a dark gray suit, white shirt, no tie—casual, understated. Tonight he strolled in with a beautiful auburn-haired woman on his arm. A stunner in a white dress leaving no doubt about the curves outlined under the soft fabric. "I'm glad you called, Dr. Bartholomew. Your table is waiting, the one in the window overlooking the harbor, as you requested."

The little man led the way as if the emperor was following in his footsteps. Barly had performed emergency heart surgery on the man's wife several years ago, saving her life. Guests glanced up as the handsome couple strolled by in the soft glow of the candles, and sparkling stemmed glassware on white linen tablecloths.

Their waiter, Carl, switched places with the maître d'. He stood at attention masking a smile as he waited to receive the doctor's drink order.

"We'll have two Manhattans?" Barly looked at Maria for her okay. She nodded in agreement. Barly added an order of crab cakes. "Oysters?"

Nodding yes, she turned back to the view of the rocky shoreline along York Harbor.

"... and two servings of your oysters. Thanks, Carl."

Carl passed the maître d' who pulled him to the side. "Carl, that woman ... with Dr. B. She looks familiar but I can't place her. The last time he was here he had a blonde on his arm. But since then he's always come alone."

Carl smiled from ear to ear. "Yes, over two years. It is the same woman."

Carl returned quickly with the drinks, the appetizers to follow in a few minutes.

"Barly ... the ocean, the rocks ... the view." She smiled. They were the same words she said before, years ago when he first brought her to the inn for dinner. He stole her heart that night but she would not admit it at the time. Turning to him, her violet eyes warm. "I love you, Dr. Bartholomew."

"Not near as much as I love you, Dr. Grayson."

Laying his hand over hers, he raised his Manhattan to hers—a musical ring as the lips of the crystal glasses touched. "Here's wishing a wonderful life for the double Ts."

"Barly, I'm making arrangements to move my mother into a home, here in York. I mentioned it to Chenoa when she and I were chatting at the cottage. She asked about my mother, and I was immediately filled with an overwhelming need to have her nearby. A place to visit, share pictures of what I'm doing ... my life. As I told Chenoa, maybe in time she'll see me as a new friend ... and if not ... well she'll be where I can look out for her."

"I like the idea, and I'd like to help." Carl set the order of oysters in front of them and, his guests indicating there was nothing more at the moment, left. Barly forked an oyster. "I have a proposal."

Maria's eyes widened. What did he mean? Oh, my God, was he going to propose we get married. Holding her breath, she waited for him to continue, watching as he dipped the oyster into the melted butter.

Barly smiled. "I met with my partners, we voted unanimously. We're offering you a partnership, head up pediatrics in our practice."

Maria's eyes dimmed ever so slightly. He watched her reaction, hoping it would be what he just saw on her face.

"Oh, my. Unanimous?"

Yeah. What do you think? Our pediatric partner is leaving in a few months. You'll have finished your residency, the kids are gone, and you'll need something to occupy your spare time."

They both chuckled. Practicing doctors have NO spare time.

"I say yes, to your proposal, Dr. Bartholomew." Holding her glass up, they toasted to her new position in his practice.

"I have another proposal."

"My, you're full of surprises tonight."

Before you start in the practice, while you're finishing your residency obligations to obtain your Pediatric license in Maine, I'd like to *propose* ...

"Yes..."

"There's a new clinic opening in Houston. The doctor, a buddy of mine from New York, called. He needs help not only with staffing but with the patients—legal babies born there from illegal parents. Many of the babies are abandoned—sometimes the mother flees back to Mexico after giving birth, other times the parents are rounded up to be deported, not claiming their babies, leaving them behind. What do you think? Want to go together?"

"Your dream! Of course, I want to go with you."

"Good." He raised his glass, another musical ring, toasting his plan. How about we have an after-dinner espresso out on the rocks, watch the waves?"

"I'd like that."

"I'll ask Carl for a couple of foam cups after we finish dinner."

———

PICKING THEIR WAY DOWN an outcropping, Barly paused. "How's this?"

"Wonderful. Did you ask Carl to add a couple of sugar cubes in our coffees?"

"Three each."

Shaking out two large dinner napkins to sit on, they leaned back on the smooth surface of the rock, the spot Barly had chosen a week ago.

They sat looking out over the waves as they crashed on the rocks below, sipping the dark, hot espresso.

Contented.

"How about you come home with me?" Barly lifted her palm to his lips.

"Well, after we see Chenoa ... I'd have to stop at the house ... pick up Jenny?"

"I wasn't talking about tonight."

Another veil of disappointment fell over her face.

"Oh ..." She glanced up.

"I mean permanently."

"Permanently? I don't know ..."

"What if we were married?"

"Well ... I suppose ..."

Barly fished in the breast pocket of his blazer. Holding a ring, he took her hand and slid it on her finger. "Maria, I'm asking you to live with me, to marry me."

Her head shook. Did she hear him right? His eyes said yes—she heard him right.

Lifting her chin, his gray eyes warm with love seeking her answer. "Marry me?"

"You proposed so many things over dinner, I'd given up, Dr. Bartholomew. You were playing a trick on me."

"This is no trick. And ... we'll have our own babies, a whole passel of babies if you want. I'm asking you to marry me, Dr. Grayson. Now, for God's sake, answer the question," he said with an impatient smile.

"Dr. Bartholomew, my answer is yes ... to all of your proposals."

———

DR. BARTHOLOMEW AND HIS new fiancée quietly entered Chenoa's dimly lit hospital room, the monitor rhythmically ticking strong and clear. Maria stepped to one side of the bed, Barly the other. Chenoa's eyes, wide open, sought her son's eyes, questioning. He nodded yes.

Turning to Maria, their hands intertwined, the ring sparkling in the monitor's light. Chenoa, lifted Maria's hand to her lips, kissing her knuckle above the ring.

Smiling, Maria bent over kissing Chenoa's cheek. "I stepped through the lens," she whispered.

Smiling, Chenoa held Maria's hand, looked down at the ring. "I'm happy for you, my dear. Happy for both of you." She looked to Barly, squeezed his hand, and turned back to Maria. "Did he tell you about the ring?"

Glancing away from Chenoa to Barly, her lips parted, questioning.

"The ring …Barly's father proposed to me, slipping that ring on my finger. I gave it to Barly before the two of you left the cottage. I told him to keep it … just in case. He was in a hurry. Didn't know what I was talking about, but accepted it. As I said, he was in a hurry so he didn't ask questions. My Joe designed it for me. Picked out the ruby, square cut, set in gold. He said the ring of diamonds around the ruby signified our abiding love for each other."

"Thank you, Chenoa. I love Barly. Loved him from when we first met but I didn't realize it, couldn't accept it until I returned, with both of you at the Moosehead cottage."

"Barly, when are you going to take this beautiful woman to be your wife?"

"We didn't get around to that, Mom. It's been a little hectic. One thing is for sure, we're waiting for you to get on your feet. Then … maybe the cottage?"

"Yes. That would be lovely. Now tell me about the children. Did they cry at leaving you?"

Barly laughed, strolled around the bed to Maria pulling her close. "Oh, yeah, Mom, they cried and cried. Maria, I'm going to sit in that chair over there while you climb up on the bed next to Mom. Get out that camera of yours and flip through the pictures over the last few hours. Please pardon me if I put my head back. Even if my eyes are closed I'll hear every word so don't leave anything out."

He kissed her lips raised to his, then put his lips to her ear. "I love you, Dr. Grayson. Remember, you said yes to all of my proposals."

The End

REVIEW REQUEST

Please consider leaving an honest review. Reader reviews are the lifeblood of any author's career. For a long-ago typewriter-jockey like myself, getting a review (especially on Amazon) means a lot.

It's easy. Log into Amazon, search for the book. **TAP** Customer Reviews at the top of the page. **Click**: Write a Customer Review.

Thank you!

Books by Mary Jane Forbes

DroneKing Trilogy
A Toy for Christmas, A Ghostly Affair
Love is in the Air

Bradley Farm Series
Bradley Farm, Sadie, Finn,
Jeli, Marshall, Georgie

The Baker Girl
One Summer, Promises

Twists of Fate Series
The Fisherman, a love story
The Witness, living a lie
Twists of Fate, daring to dream

Murder by Design, Series:
Murder by Design, Labeled in Seattle
Choices

Elizabeth Stitchway, PI, Series
The Mailbox, Black Magic,
The Painter, Twister

House of Beads Mystery Series
Murder in the House of Beads
Intercept, Checkmate, Identity Theft

Novels - standalone
The Baby Quilt, The Message

Short Stories
Once Upon a Christmas Eve, a Romantic Fairy Tale
The Christmas Angel and the Magic Holiday Tree

Visit: www.MaryJaneForbes.com